A SPY PRINCESS

A Sweet Fantasy Romance

THE DANCING PRINCESSES
BOOK IV

ALEA HENLE

CRABGRASS PUBLISHING

ISBN: 978-1-952735-19-6 (e-book), 978-1-952735-20-2 (print)

Published by Crabgrass Publishing

Editing by Rare Bird Editing.

Cover design by Augusta Scarlett

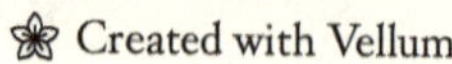 Created with Vellum

Trouble never arrived alone, always as part of a pair. Other members of the court, servants and courtiers, laughed at the notion. Considered it provincial, the kind of thing only someone from one of the tiny towns in the hinterlands might swallow.

Emmi saw no reason not to admit her superstitions and even embrace them. She didn't walk around proclaiming her worries of paired troubles—but she sought out odd numbers wherever possible. She made certain she wore an odd number of clothes: a simple cloth tied around her privates, another supporting her generous breasts, and a plain gray tunic over. The worn hem hit her mid-calf, almost the same color as her taupe skin. Smooth leather sandals covered her feet, tied on with ribbons that wrapped up past the hem. Soft black hair with purple undertones swung around her face, kept short to be less trouble—and save time to be used elsewhere.

The soft gray and yellow striped mantle draped over her tunic complemented her coloring, but also had the insignia of the court woven into the center marking her as an attendant. Valued, of course, for the rulers and most courtiers recognized they wouldn't function without servants, but still one of those who worked mostly in the back halls, particularly at the summer palace complex with its dozens of buildings, hundreds of stairways, and thousands of rooms, whether within walls or plazas open to the air.

Emmi loved the quarter of the year spent at the summer palace. Some might complain about the heat and humidity, and the risk of the horrendous storms that blew up across the lake at the peak of the summer, but not her. True, even this late in the summer sweat slicked her skin and made her hair cling to the sides of her head. But the wide windows placed even, or especially, in stairwells caught and directed breezes to ensure moisture was regularly wicked away.

More important than heat: her closest sibling worked here, having fallen in love with the area. Emmi's place attending at court allowed her to visit with him every year and carry word back to their family in a small town near the northern capital.

Like her brother, Emmi loved how the southern capital burst with color. Nearly every wall bore some type of adornment, usually mosaics formed of myriad tiles that portrayed nature or history. Matching colored stones formed intricate patterns covering the floors. The public rooms always boasted at least one scene of a previous Terparchon or Marchon conquering this territory or making that decree. The back halls were better—brightened with jungles and forests teeming with animal and bird life, or underwater scenes in lakes and rivers showing one array of colorful fish and snails after another.

The stairways might not have mosaics, but they were whitewashed and then painted and repainted, always with different colors and patterns. Giggles and the smell of paint rose from one story below, where the denizens of the children's palace spent the morning hours decorating. Emmi had stopped by for a few moments earlier, and listened to her seven-year-old daughter explain that the tall-eared purple blob she drew was actually a fish with three tails.

A fish who'd last on the stairs for a year or more, delighting—or, more likely, confusing—anyone who noticed. Susa's current best friend, the child of the Terparchon's Chief Accountant, painted a rainbow snail nearby. All children played together regardless of their parents' station, because, as the Terparchon had pointed out more than once in Emmi's hearing, who could tell what a child would be until they were grown? Much as Emmi loved order and tidiness, she preferred her daughter have a world of possibilities before her. There were good reasons she'd left her village to take service, no matter that she still sometimes missed home.

And people who understood that a bad thing that came alone was only waiting for its match to follow.

Emmi counted the steps when climbing to ensure the third floor of the northern administrative hall remained exactly twenty-three above the first. Everything in its place—order above chaos. Her lungs protested the speed with which she'd climbed, so she paused at the top. Tightened the light-blue cord around her waist, adjusting the ends so that they swayed against her hip rather than her front.

No stains marred the fabric, though bits of dust clung to the hem. She'd been summoned halfway through cleaning out the rooms of the three princesses she regularly waited on. Careful with a broom she might be, but one couldn't escape dust.

And she hadn't been allowed time to go back to her rooms to change. The thin, fair-skinned eleee who'd come for her had sworn they were told to take over her tasks—without specifying whether for the morning or permanently. They'd nearly grabbed the broom out of her hand! Then sent her on her way with a smile.

The kind of look that said *better you than me.*

Small wonder she sought out odds to ward off trouble. As she walked down the hall, she brushed her fingers along the nine doors lining the left side, matched on the right but with an extra at the far end to ensure they totaled twenty-one. Transom windows above each door were all partly opened, ensuring ample circulation of warm air.

A glance ahead at the open door of the palacekeeper who oversaw the servants who cleaned, mended, and tended, showed only one person present: Desma herself.

The room seemed small with Desma in it, although it was almost the size of the lesser princess chambers in their hall. Of medium height and breadth, Desma had brown hair liberally streaked with gray, brown eyes, light brown skin, and round features topped by a snub nose.

Every element of Desma's appearance, from polished sandals to light yellow tunic to brighter mantle with the court insignia, individually was unremarkable. The whole somehow became memorable, and Desma stood out whenever she ventured into the royal reception areas as readily as she did against the bare whitewashed walls. The chamber held a table and a stool on either side. Shelves affixed to the wall behind supported assorted piles of scrap paper, several chalk boards, and broken nubs of chalk.

The table held more scraps of paper—and a carafe of spiced water with two dinged bronze goblets.

The presence of refreshment and enough cups made Emmi nervous. So too did the kind but wry twist to Desma's thin lips.

Emmi accepted a glass of water as she perched on a stool, not daring to so much as offer to pour it herself. The metal was cool to the touch, already beading with perspiration indicating the water had started with ice. A single chilly sip, and she set it down with care and awaited her fate.

"How are you and your princesses?" Desma always began with the same question, at least for Emmi ever since she'd come to Desma's attention in the first place and risen to attend princesses. But perhaps Desma had less of a smile than other times?

Or maybe Emmi worried over air fears. "All's well. No troubles to report."

Not in her work. Her daughter complained about the upcoming progress and having to leave Yaras and her beloved uncle-aunt. Emmi's sibling, in turn, regularly bent her ear about her lack of love life. Much as she loved him, he regularly suggested the most unsuitable candidates with whom to break her years-long fast. This one because he had a nice smile, that one had such a neat swing to their hips. Even a man notable mostly for having serenaded a different woman at midnight outside the hall Emmi lived in, waking her daughter and every other child in the building and resulting in cranky parents the next morning.

If anything, serving the princesses offered Emmi a respite from family drama. She was fortunate that the princesses were all easy to please and did much for themselves—yet still appreciated the order and tidiness that Emmi brought to their lives.

With the occasional bobble, but that was only to be expected.

"Gisela is still surprised and a bit uneasy with my keeping her rooms tidy." Emmi winced. The newest princess hadn't fully adjusted to having a servant attend her clothes and chambers. "But she always thanks me for arranging for food and water and having her clothes cleaned. Though I did find her once trying to wash out a mantle herself."

Desma shuddered. "Tell me it was a plain one."

Emmi shook her head. Even the plain dancing tunics of the princesses required a special degree of care to ensure they didn't wear out too fast or get mixed up between sizes, but the mantles with embroidery or fringe needed even more cautious laundering, when they couldn't be spot-cleaned. "No, but she hasn't tried again since."

"Good. I'll have a word with her, if necessary." Desma lifted her cup and made a toast to absent princesses. "But it is so much simpler if they just accept that good laundering requires skilled labor as well as strength. I needn't ask if Jola or Heron has tried to clean their clothes lately."

"They never would. Of course Jola is rarely in her room anyway, and doesn't require that much assistance from me these days."

"That is a consideration for reallocating assignments." Desma nodded. "I know you've lent a hand many times to your fellows in keeping up with their princesses."

Both were well aware of where Jola spent most of her days and nights, in royal chambers with her lover. Just one reason Emmi was able to pitch in and help others.

"And Heron?"

"They're as lovely to serve as ever." Emmi folded her hands in her lap, hoping no blush stained her cheeks. She'd helped Heron, a stranger made princess, adjust to Codaros in their first years. Explaining Codaros customs while she cleaned had grown into a tradition of trading stories several times a week.

"Good, though I am not surprised." Desma made a note on a scrap of paper. "They've been part of court long enough to know the rules. Gisela will learn, she seems intelligent enough."

Emmi nodded, waiting for the trouble to descend.

Desma stared down at the paper in front of her. It had many lines written, half crossed out, and nearly all impossible to read upside-down no matter how Emmi tried.

The other woman said nothing, letting the pause spiral out into something bigger until Emmi couldn't handle the quiet.

"Is there any change to the splitting of the court?" Emmi asked. "There are so many rumors going around that there will be three small courts rather than two this year."

"Rumor does seem to have the right of it this time, but that needn't trouble you." Desma set her stylus down and clasped hands. "I can say no more at this time, but you will be following the Marchon's train on southern and eastern progress."

South. Warmer and slower than the north, for Emmi had enough experience with both. If she had a preference it was the south. Beautiful, hot, and with some slow, rough patches through the occasional jungle, and lots of hilly country.

"You're doing excellent work." Desma smiled, showing her teeth. "I wish I had more such as you in employ."

"Yes?"

"You handle three princesses with ease, sometimes as many as five in a pinch, with no difficulties. Alas, I have other staff unable to care for a single person."

Dread roiled in Emmi's belly. She took a second sip of spiced water, but it did nothing to ease her nerves. The cup rocked when she returned it to the table, despite her care.

"I need you to switch for the fall progress. We can reconsider when we reach the winter palace, if necessary, but not before."

Of course Desma would follow the Terparchon's progress to the north. That part made sense, even though one of Desma's deputies would accompany the southern progress and be able to make changes. But whatever Emmi was to take on, Desma didn't want her abandoning it early or at all.

"Switch to . . ." Emmi started, only to trail off.

Desma's smile still showed her teeth, but her gaze turned pensive. "It's not a big change, from three princesses to a single compeer—and a royal compeer at that!"

A royal compeer? There were three, four if one counted the

Marchon, but surely he wouldn't need Emmi. He had an attendant who'd served him as long as Emmi had been at court. As for his and the Terparchon's children, each had mixed reputations among the lower halls. The elder daughter, Nefeli, was a born compeer and always knew where people were, which could be a bit unnerving. Todor, the middle child, had memory issues and reputedly would tell one servant something and assume others knew it. Zora, the younger daughter, tended to lose things and throw fits until they were found.

"Who?" Emmi asked.

"Zora." Desma reached over and patted Emmi's hand. "You can tell your princesses today that you're leaving them, and first thing tomorrow we'll make the change. I'll assign a fine attendant or two to take over with them, and I'll show you around Zora's chambers myself."

"Do I have a choice?" Emmi racked her memory for tales of Zora from the servants' halls. Surprisingly few, other than her possessiveness.

"Emmi." Was that a plea in Desma's voice? "I'm near the end of possibilities. Zora's previous attendant suited for years, but reached her thirty while on the spring march and retired. Since then, she's gone through . . . nine attendants."

"Nine?" Two or three might be understandable after such a long time with the same person, but thrice that number said a lot about a person.

"No one has lasted a full moon." Desma sighed.

"What happened?" At three or four moons total since the retirement, most wouldn't have even lasted a half-moon.

"Didn't like the condition of her rooms, didn't like her reaction to them tidying, complaints of inconsistency—of her asking for things and then countermanding the orders or denying she'd given them—and dislike of her, er, companions." Desma counted off on her fingers. "On the other side, complaints of prying, unreliability, sticking their noses where they weren't wanted."

And Desma wanted Emmi to wade into this and make it all right?

"You're the most capable person I have." Desma laid her hands flat on the table. "There are one or two attendants back at Tharis who might do to sub in when we get there, though no promises, but at a minimum I need someone to see to her on the autumn progress who can stick with it—no complaints on either side. I have no one else with the experience, the subtlety, the diplomacy."

"Experience?" Many others with far more years service than Emmi, plus ample subtlety and diplomacy.

"You have a sibling who's a multiple, don't you?"

"Yes." Emmi sat back, gripping the edge of the stool. That was why Desma wanted her? "You think that's why she's hard to please? But my brother-sister is the sweetest, kindest person I know."

"It might help," Desma said. "I don't know how many people Zora is, but some of them are harder to deal with than others, and your familiarity . . ."

Emmi tried to offer alternatives, but Desma had an objection for every one. It was a polite fiction between them, Desma offering Emmi the illusion of choice. They both knew in the end she'd have to accept the change.

No matter how Emmi considered the matter, even though the new position came with a pay raise, it was a piece of bad news.

One, no doubt, with the match waiting around a corner to pounce.

Still, Emmi was allowed to tell her current princesses. She'd have a last exchange with one in particular, who'd been a painful joy to wait upon. One last time to look on Heron close up, talk to them about their day, see them smile just for her.

Then never again.

❦   2   ❦

Even after five years, Heron paused a few steps into their rooms and wondered if they'd made a wrong turn. They turned around, sandals squeaking against the clean floor and the bright green skirts of their tunic flaring around their light brown calves except where the heavier weight of the matching mantle hung down along their side. The angle of the sunlight turned Heron's gilded toenails full gold. After a second round, everything settled and turned familiar.

But also, always, strange.

Every time they considered the matter, they discovered new, subtle differences between the chambers allotted to them in the summer palace of Codaros and those in the far-off city-state of Kitiva, where they'd grown up and spent the first half of their lives.

The very proportions of the outer, receiving chamber were wrong. Despite Heron's being taller than most, the ceilings soared nearly an arm's length above their head. A rectangular window above the door pulled a light draft from the window, ensuring the warm, moist air kept moving.

Kitivans would consider this oppressively hot high summer weather, but here it was merely the usual temperature for early evening at the end of summer. From the vantage of five summers in Codaros—following seven times as many in Kitiva—Heron agreed with both vantage points simultaneously, although their body had somewhat adjusted. The sweat lining their skin had already begun to dry, despite recent labors including a demonstration dance down in the city and lengthy walk back to palace after.

The rooms' contents also gave them pause. Two couches formed an L, positioned to catch the cooling draft. Although piled high with cushions, Heron had yet to quite figure out why everyone in this part of the land considered reclining more comfortable than sitting in a proper chair—especially to eat. Thousands of tiny colored tiles covered the walls and floor with fantastical images of wheels and impossible fields featuring full-grown plants that in truth flowered at different times. Beautiful, yes, but sometimes they longed for plain walls adorned at most with one or two small framed paintings of places or people.

Or even nothing at all.

No fireplace or any means of keeping the room warm, of course, not that they'd ever spent the winter here.

Shutting their eyes did nothing to dispel the differences, for long bird calls echoed in the distance. Birds who never ventured up the river from the great lake, and thus were never heard in Kitiva.

Yet alongside the strangeness was familiarity. As usual, everything in its place just as when they'd left earlier in the day. Emmi had passed through to clean, given the absence of dust and the full pitchers of water on the table between the couches and visible through the archway into the smaller sleeping chamber. Likewise, the carefully folded clean cloths on a shelf by the door and no doubt more with their clean clothes lining the bedroom shelves. Their dirty laundry taken away, leaving the clear, pure scent of the lavender sachets carefully scattered to keep away pests.

Bending, they undid the straps on their sandals and dropped them into the low, long, wide-mouthed basket holding the rest of their dozen-odd pairs.

These were the same rooms Heron had occupied summer after summer, when the Codaros court settled into Yaras for three moons at a stretch. They knew how to find their way around, although they still sometimes got lost in the warren of halls, buildings, gardens, and open-air plazas that formed the summer palace.

Five years of this predictability, of being on the move as a dancing princess. They accompanied the rulers when the court followed the regular circuit in the same rounds, always spending the summer on the lake and the winter high near the mountains to the north, and splitting to progress through the remainder of the land during spring and autumn.

Better in many ways than their life before. They preferred knowing where they'd go next, and having duties focused around practicing moves and performing Dances that helped keep land and people safe from torrential storms, wildfires, and other natural disasters.

They'd worked as a messenger, trader, and spy. Once grown, they'd never known where they'd be sent next. Never remained in their home city long enough to lease regular rooms rather than squatting in whatever boarding house had an opening they could afford. Never found a lover they were able to stay close to for more than a season.

Who wouldn't prefer being part of court, in a position guaranteed a pension and thus rarely having to worry about finding coins?

Nevertheless, at home they never felt like a stranger. They always counted as a citizen, albeit an awkward one who didn't quite fit in when they opened their mouth but was still "one of us."

Versus walking into a room called theirs, and needing a moment to blink before recognizing it.

Grabbing a towel from the door, they wiped down their face and squeezed bits of moisture from their shoulder-length hair.

Why such a reverie? It wasn't as though anything changed from the morning or the previous day or the day before that. Usually, after the moment's pause and blink, they moved on with little thought.

Except a hint of pine hung in the air, almost but not quite hidden under the lavender. More, it wasn't the kind of pine scent emanating from the related trees growing this far south, but the heart pines that only grew in the mountains further north.

Or was that their imagination?

They shook and stretched. Muscles crackled, but remained warm and flexible despite residual aches from practice in the morning and the exhibition in the city earlier, for residents of a small neighborhood. The latter hadn't ended well. A fellow princess showed signs of burnout, thus giving Heron a glimpse of their future. Then again, the other princess seemed determined to press on and dance to the last step, which Heron would not do. They would step aside when their day came, and . . . figure out something new to do.

Or maybe go home, if Kitiva remained home after the years away.

Hardly comfortable thoughts.

Shaking their head, they padded into the bedroom. The narrow wooden bedstead, at least, was relatively similar to the beds of Kitiva, although the thick mattress was lavishly stuffed with lavender-scented grass where the beds they'd slept on in the past used wool or pine needles, and much less of it.

A thin linen blanket covered mattress and lumpy pillows, woven with five wide stripes alternating green and red. Shelves rather than mosaics covered most of the walls, bearing an array of tunics and mantles suited to all manner of occasions and weather, plus undergarments and the accoutrements of their rank.

They pulled off the mantle and hung it on a peg to dry. The sweaty tunic went in the laundry basket.

A narrow, oblong memory keeper hung from a cord around their neck. The thick blue cloth was worked with a single silver star, the spikes extending to the edges. Wrapping a hand around it brought a sensation akin to being held and pressed at the center of a mass of loved ones.

Pouring lukewarm water into a bowl, they dipped in a clean cloth and sponged themselves off, careful not to wet the memory keeper any more. Although waterproofed, such protection was known to fade and crack over time.

Only then, drying in the low, warm draft, did they notice a wide leaf resting atop the bed. Whoever had placed it there had carefully aligned it with the green streak at the center. The colors were similar, the leaf being a tad lighter, but the serrated edges lapped over onto the red stripes to either side.

The leaf came from a tree which didn't grow around here. It didn't smell of pine, but as Heron drew close their nostrils twitched at the faint hint of mold. When they poked the leaf, it proved soft but dry. Pliable, albeit starting to fray and disintegrate along the edges.

All the same, it remained suitable for writing on—and someone had.

Jerky, thick symbols formed a single line down the center of the leaf. No salutation, no compliments or kindnesses: just the time and place to meet and reasons to assume that Heron would cooperate.

After all Heron had done, all they'd provided, surely little remained to ask of them. They didn't have access to any secrets except details of the Dances they participated in. The Terparchon had made that clear when she'd offered Heron a place. Even desperate to keep the number of princesses at twelve, not counting her, she wouldn't invite them in if it endangered her land.

Heron had passed the news along. Bent in the end and given what they could when they could, but nothing remained. Certainly nothing justifying being contacted in the south when they never had before.

What couldn't wait until Heron returned north?

They jerked and nearly squashed the leaf at the sudden knock at the door.

"Heron?" The door and the distance between Heron and the door couldn't muffle Emmi's lovely, breathy voice.

"Just a moment," they called. Leaping into action, they stuffed the leaf out of sight. Under a pile of clean tunics—not the best choice, but Emmi had already tidied so surely she wouldn't notice.

They grabbed the first tunic at hand, no matter how plain, and donned it but left it loose and unbelted. A quick brush of a hand against the base of their neck ensured the memory keeper hung beneath the cloth. While not a secret, better to keep it covered.

When they turned, the bits of leaf broken off from the edges proved far more noticeable than the whole leaf had been. The speckles of green and brown practically glowed against the stripes. Emmi couldn't miss them if she came this far.

Heron hastily swept them off, but they stood out against the tiled floor, too. Kicking them under the bed would have to do. Surely Emmi wouldn't consider them odd when she swept in the morning.

Wiping sweat from their forehead with back of hand, they went to open the door.

Emmi smiled from the other side of a small, wheeled cart, as beautiful as ever. Perhaps others didn't consider her the same, for Heron had never heard her name mentioned among the beauties of the court. For that matter, Heron had barely noticed her appearance their first confusing year at court. Yet over the succeeding seasons, they'd come to the conclusion that no one else had such a sweetly curved smile, or brown eyes that lit so charmingly, or the same tilt to their head that made a lock of black hair fall to the center and beg to be tucked back.

Or such curves beneath their simple tunic and mantle that deserved to be stroked and adored. Heron tucked their hands behind their back to resist the urge to touch—even no more than a pat on the shoulder or back, something welcome and expected in Kitiva but forbidden in Codaros without express permission.

"May I?" Emmi asked.

Glad that no one ever seemed to notice when they flushed, Heron stood back.

Her words offered a fresh reminder that they hadn't figured out how people in Codaros courted each other—there seemed such strange varieties—only what was frowned upon. The latter, alas, included a strong prohibition against abusing rank.

"I heard you returned from the city, and thought you might like some refreshments, since you missed dinner." She rolled the cart in and shifted the contents to a low table between the couches. The platter of sliced starmeg and peppers arranged around a bowl of spiced yogurt overrode any other scents.

So often she guessed what they might need before they had a chance to request. Their stomach rumbled, reminded they hadn't eaten in a while.

"Thank you." Heron sat, feet firm on the floor although the low height of the couch forced their knees up toward their chest. "You take such kind care."

"It's been a pleasure." She blushed, ducking her head to the side. "I've always enjoyed caring for princesses. I don't like having favorites, but, if I did you'd be one."

More kindness, and such a lovely color on her cheeks, down along the sides of her neck, and slipping under her striped tunic. How much further might it go? They squashed such thoughts as unfitting. The one absolute thing they had been warned about was to never touch anyone who worked for them.

They ducked their head instead, only to find bits of leaf stuck to their tunic. More clung to their right hand, green against brown.

Emmi spoke, but only the sound of her voice registered. No words.

Had she noticed the leaf bits? Or, with her tidy nature, she might catch that the pile of tunics in the bedroom—visible through the archway—wasn't as straight and neat as she'd left it. Heron should have picked a less visible spot, but they'd rushed.

No one had noticed their clandestine correspondence with their homeland over the years. If anyone had, they'd kept the secret from Heron. Safer to worry about the latter, but they hoped the former.

Unless, had *Emmi* left the leaf so carefully aligned on the bed? There was no reason for her to do so. She, of all people, had every excuse to hand items to Heron, not hide them.

If she hadn't, then whoever had must have waited until after Emmi had finished cleaning the room. In which case they'd gone to efforts to keep it from her. Wise, for Emmi was the one person who'd caught them once or twice writing out missives to be sent on. Without reading over their shoulder, or they thought, had thought, but they'd needed to get her away before she did notice.

Just in case.

"This is wonderful, I appreciate it very much." Heron hid their right hand in the folds of their tunic, clutching fabric to hide the bits of leaf. With their left, they picked up a slice of starmeg and dipped it in the yogurt. "Lovely, as always."

Though the taste soured the instant it hit their belly.

"I'm glad." Emmi nodded and left, with one last glance back before shutting the door.

Why did she look so disappointed?

❧ 3 ❧

Emmi's head ached. Or her heart, but she focused on her head and gave her temples a few rubs. The sun had just vanished behind the hills on the far side of the lake, thankfully. No more blinding reflections on the water. Instead, hints of pink and orange began to streak the sky. The air turned cooler, verging on chilly.

Boulders lined both sides of the path along the shore, some there from the start and others rolled to discourage people from leaving the path and wandering up the hillside straight toward the palace. Emmi pulled her mantle tighter around her shoulders, hunched on a suitable boulder.

The light breeze kicked up small waves that slapped the rocky shore and carried the spray far enough inland to dampen Emmi's toes, making her colder.

In contrast, Emmi's daughter, Susa, didn't mind getting wet. Her tunic clung to her knees as she stood in the middle of the path, halfway between Emmi and the water. Every few minutes, Susa got too close to the waves. Each time she got one loud harrumph warning and shifted back. With a glint in her eye, those dark eyes she'd gotten from her father, and that same mulish tilt to the chin at being thwarted.

The silky straight hair she'd got from Emmi, and the narrow nose, and most of the rest they'd have to wait until she finished growing to decide what came from whom and what was Susa's alone. Time enough to argue it over then.

Susa bent and scrabbled to pry another thin stone from the hard-packed earth. The seventh? Eighth? Her fingers would be all mud for days, but there were worse things.

The girl's haste, on the other hand . . . as soon as she freed the stone, she whirled around and tried to skip it across the waves, but it sank with a faint plop. Same as all the others. Emmi had offered pointers with the first through third, and been shrugged off, so might as well sit and wait.

Given the hectic color rising in Susa's cheeks, getting her away from the lake and off to bed wouldn't be easy. For the moment, though, she took pleasure in tossing stones and required little more than her mother watching.

Unfortunately, that just gave Emmi more time to think about how messy her life had become.

Untidiness, exactly what she least liked. Susa would grow out of it eventually, surely. What child of seven didn't whirl from wonderful to awful in a breath? The girl had cleaned up the pieces of the pitcher she'd dropped on purpose, and done a good enough job Emmi had agreed to this evening venture.

As for Emmi's sibling sticking his nose into her business and trying to spice up her life, she'd get away from him when the court left. Then spend the next months missing his good qualities, and his knack in baking the pastries she loved most.

Usually work balanced the rest out, providing reward by allowing Emmi to make messy things tidy, turn disorder into order and cleanliness—and earn a decent living at the same time.

Emmi had thought the princesses she served appreciated her labors.

Gisela and Jola had both been very nice and sad about Emmi's reassignment. They'd miss her and wished her well, and that was that. Granted, Gisela had asked if Emmi would show her how to clean mantles, but accepted when Emmi insisted her replacement would arrange for laundry. They provided cleanliness, even as Gisela's princess magic helped keep the land and people safe.

But Heron had been so strange, so abrupt and distant, as if they didn't care.

Maybe they didn't. Yet Emmi had serviced their rooms ever since they first became a princess! But Heron had shared some things about their homeland over the years, and they reckoned fives as special numbers. Perhaps they considered Emmi's reassignment a normal course of events.

Emmi preferred that to the alternative that crept into her mind and refused to be dislodged. Heron had also mentioned other differences between Kitiva and Codaros, though most of their interest was in how to adapt to life in Codaros. Still, Emmi had picked up the suggestion that Kitivans considered cleaning the kind of work anyone could do and therefore not worth much.

Heron had never made her feel that way.

Until now.

With a shriek of joy, Susa freed another pebble from the path and flung it into the lake. Then gave a shriek of fury at the plop. Jaw set, she squatted down and dug her fingers in again.

Emmi started to rise, setting her teeth and getting ready to dig in herself and pry Susa from the lake.

The slap of sandals against the path had her turning about instead. After an instant's tension, Emmi relaxed as her sibling turned the corner and tromped over to settle on a boulder next to Emmi with a huff.

Anyone and everyone could guess Aurel and Emmi were related, for they shared the same straight black hair, although he wore it longer, halfway down his back. The same brown eyes in a round, taupe face. Small nose, way of walking, even the same general height and stance, although he was otherwise broad and straight with a slight paunch pushing out his gray tunic under his blue mantle, while she curved out and in and out again.

There was no one else—almost—she'd want sitting next to her under most circumstances.

The only sticking point was to figure out which of her siblings had come to find her, since four selves shared the one body. Most likely, the new arrival was her winklingly officious older brother who was thoroughly responsible and hence usually in control. Or perhaps the impish "Rellie" who sometimes played games with Susa for hours. Alternatively, the visitor might be Auri, the sole female, who liked to meddle and found Emmi a suitable object no matter how often or loudly Emmi protested. The fourth rarely showed. Emmi wasn't sure she'd ever met him, but Aurel said he existed and who would know better?

"You're up late," Emmi said.

"So's Susa." Aurel leaned over to give Emmi a hug, then sat up straight with his hands atop his belly. The fabric there was clean, for once, with no sign of flour, though he smelled of baking and sweet sauces all the same. He'd likely napped after his early shift in the kitchens, and donned a clean tunic before coming in search of her. A compliment, or effort to avoid her cleaning his clothes with him still in them, even if she'd only done that once under great duress. "She'll be a pain to rouse tomorrow morning if you don't get her down soon."

"She had a good nap earlier." Emmi nodded at the clean fabric.

He pretended not to notice, nodding in turn at the girl squatting in the path. "Still, your daughter's no morning bird. She gets grouchy when she doesn't have enough sleep."

"The same is true of you, so why are you here?"

"A little bird told me you might be wanting me." Aurel angled so that he could watch her and Susa at once.

"A bird?" Emmi crossed her arms over her chest and tapped her fingers against her shoulders.

"Very well, then, not a bird." Aurel shrugged. "Your boss."

"You know her?" Emmi asked, sure he'd take the meaning right: that he'd talked to Desma, not merely that he was aware of Desma's existence. Large though the court was, most people had a general sense of who others were whether or not they ever interacted.

"She likes what I cook. Asks me for things special sometimes."

"Ah ha." Emmi looked him over and shook her head. He was good looking enough, but she couldn't quite see him with Desma, not to mention Emmi's supervisor had a partner and two children.

"No, no, it's not like that. Not at all. But Desma's done turns over seeing palace kitchens, supplies, and logistics, and now she supervises attendants." Aurel nodded at Emmi. "I wouldn't be surprised to see her getting up to be one of the Terparchon's chief domestic advisers one of these days."

"Agreed."

"So of course I know her," he said. "And she seemed to think you might want to talk to me."

"Did she tell you why?" Emmi grimaced as Susa heaved another pebble into the lake with no more success at skipping. This time the girl dropped down to sit on the earth she'd already dug through as she pursued another stone. More mud to clean off her later.

"Some. She's talked to me before about the matter." He laid a finger across his lips. "Neither of us naming any names or saying anything too specific in case the flowers or stones have ears."

"Or certain others present." Emmi nodded at her daughter, although the child didn't seem to pay attention to anything but the pursuit of another pebble.

"Or her especially, since she's the age and temperament that anything she thinks spills out of her mouth sooner or later." Aurel grimaced. "At any rate, Desma came to me as I'm the most upfront at court about being many in one. There are others, but most don't want to talk about it, some not even to me, any of me. She thought that might give her insights, though I had to tell her it didn't, because no one's ever the same, no matter how many selves we're talking."

"I could've told her that." Emmi said. And had, too, although apparently after Aurel had done so.

"Though it doesn't hurt you've got a good record of figuring out who's in charge of me even when one of me tries to hide it."

"It's not always that hard." She guessed half the time, though she wasn't going to tell him, them, that. Apparently her guesses were better than she'd thought.

"All else being the same, I might've said that you've got a good way of dealing with all of me. You don't do much more than blink if we make a switch, or one of me forgets to tell another something, such as the time you—" He slapped a hand over his mouth. The last words had risen to almost a squeak, possibly Rellie peeking through. Usually Emmi only talked to one of them, but sometimes more showed up.

Emmi ignored the cut off thought in favor of what Aurel had openly admitted: suggesting Desma ask Emmi to make a change. She pulled her mantle more tightly around her shoulders as the sky darkened above and the first stars began to glimmer through. "So I've got you to thank for this."

"Your name had already come up, but she'd avoided changing up people with long-standing positions taking care of this that or the other persons." Aurel started, then blinked and tilted his head to the side as his voice gained a mellow, teasing edge. Auri said, "and yes, I suggested you might be ready for a change, so you're welcome."

Emmi glared at Auri, who only smiled more.

"The change'll be good for you, too." Auri waved at the shadows farther along the lake path. "Get you away from a certain person."

A long, lanky figure in a gray tunic and mantle, more limbs than torso, headed along a different path up from the copse of trees where the shore cut into the lake. Despite the distance, Emmi couldn't mistake that body or way of walking.

"Why?" Emmi asked.

"Because I love you and even when you're not talking to me because of this, that, or the other, I've ears to hear how you talk about *them* this last year, no matter that no one else seems to." Auri slipped over to sit next to Emmi and wrap arms around her shoulders, although the two of them didn't fit and Emmi had to dig her heels against the earth to keep from slipping off.

This close, the shift of personality rippled through Emmi as her sibling's voice dropped back down.

"I heard it too," Aurel said. After a brief squeak "and me!" from Rellie, Aurel continued "you've been sighing for them for years. It's time you got a move on to something else, or someone else able to look back at you the way you look at them."

"Meddler." Emmi tensed her calves and pushed back.

Aurel thumped off the boulder onto the path, legs and arms sprawling as he grinned at her. "Guilty, but hey, at least you'll be free of me until next spring."

"No!!" Susa scrambled to her knees. Pausing, she waited for Aurel's nod before crawling over to grab as much of him as she could. "I don't wanna leave you—"

"You're not leaving anyone yet, Susa darling." Emmi swung down to lift Susa by the shoulders and hug her dirt and all, in vain hope to head off an incipient tantrum.

"Don't make me go." The girl wiggled, elbows hitting Emmi's arms and sides. "I wanna stay with uncle-aunt!"

"Just you? Not your Ma too?" Rellie asked, pushing up onto his knees. Aurel took control right after, since Rellie would never have started dusting himself off but done something more drastic instead.

"I'll thank you to keep your help to yourself." Emmi frowned at him, stroking her daughter's hair as best she could. "Maybe next year you can stay here, Susa, but now it's time for bed. And guess what? Uncle-aunt has offered to tuck you in and tell you a story!"

The girl stopped wriggling. She sniffed, a few tears trickling down her cheeks. Then yawned wide and slid from Emmi's grasp to lean against Aurel. "Two stories?"

"Oh, joy." Aurel picked Susa up and swung her high before setting her back on her feet and urging her to start back toward the rooms Emmi and Susa shared, close by his. "One story."

"Two? Please, please, please?"

He threw a desperate glance over his shoulder.

Emmi smiled. "Meddle in my life and I'll meddle in yours."

She followed sibling and daughter along the path, away from the copse and the familiar lanky figure. Yet when she reached the turn that would take her out of sight, she paused long enough to glance behind.

A dark, lanky shadow on the hill gazed back.

❧ 4 ❧

Heron ate lightly after Emmi left dinner with them. They leaned against the couch cushions, trying to ignore an itchy sensation between their shoulder blades. Reaching back to scratch did nothing to dispel the prickling. The room seemed emptier without Emmi. She sometimes lingered after bringing meals by, starting to tidy while Heron was still in the room, which allowed them to talk. Without listening ears around, or judgmental eyes fixed on them, they could ask about the many ways life in Codaros differed from Kitiva, and get honest, trustworthy answers—and in return offer anecdotes from their day and their adventures before becoming a princess.

Something missing this evening.

Though Heron couldn't share the rest of the evening's adventures with Emmi. The little they'd eaten turned sour in their belly, and they left the rest on the platter. A cup of water didn't help, perhaps because the water retained a chill from the slivers of ice floating in it, and the cool made the sour worse.

Or it might all be nerves.

Heron's fingers fumbled as they belted their tunic and donned the mantle least likely to attract notice—a soft gray with subtle trim of entwined vines in silver and gold. Plain sandals only half-worn through went on their feet, the ties fastened at their ankles.

Still in the bedroom, they opened the narrow box that held their chains, cords, and circlets of office. Slipping fingers along the side, they extracted a small square of folded parchment and tucked it under their belt.

Then removed the leaf from beneath the tunics and reviewed the message one last time.

The flowery symbol scratched at the top represented Kitiva and Kitivan citizens' loyalty to the city no matter where they roamed. For those who lived elsewhere, it encapsulated their connection to Kitiva and responsibilities as citizens no matter how far they roamed.

Below lay a bisected heart, denoting family and sacrifice—an implicit reminder that Heron had family still living in Kitiva, though their parents had died several years earlier. Their family and friends might be called on to pay any debts to the city that Heron failed to honor.

In addition, the leaf indicated the time and place to meet. Show up tonight at sunset, with tomorrow as backup should the weather prove inclement, or allowed in the event Heron found the message too late.

The familiar handwriting suggested Heron would meet same man as usual: their uncle, Stork. The Kitivan council was parsimonious, and preferred to set family to keep their relatives up to the mark wherever possible.

Nothing in the leaf explained why Stork had ventured so far south, although as a trader of oddities he often changed his routes to discover new trinkets. Stork had evidently stayed in the area long enough to figure out a remote place to meet: the oak grove where the land jutted briefly out into the lake, the only part of the palace gardens shared with the city.

Stork could wander there relatively easily, especially if he stayed in an inn close to the shore.

Heron would have to pass through a gate, and give their name to the palace guard, who would write it down if anyone cared to check the records later.

This stood as yet another variance from their usual meetings, designed to appear as semi-accidental encounters in the crowded city markets of Tharis during the busiest parts of the day.

Why the rush? The leaf gave no answers, only raised questions.

Heron crumpled the leaf, grinding it down and mixing the bits with the leftover yogurt until they had a green, goopy mess. They set the unfinished dinner dishes just outside the door for pickup. Doing so offered an opportunity to check and see if the hall was clear of company—no other princesses or their friends hanging around to notice them leaving.

Empty though the corridor was, they strolled as though merely out for an evening stroll and their insides were not roiling.

Down the stairs. Out the door. Then, they created a winding, twisty-turny path to the far wall and the gate leading to the oak grove.

Heron left the comfortable surroundings provided by the ruler who'd welcomed them into her group of dancing princesses and trusted them to help maintain the well-being of the land through the magical Dances.

This, even though Heron came from a rival city across the river.

"Why me?" they'd asked the Terparchon that fateful day, still reeling from having discovered they'd unknowingly sprouted princess magic, news broken to them when the Terparchon had asked them to join in a desperate effort to ease and soothe an immense blizzard threatening the city. She'd barely allowed Heron to recover from that first Dance before summoning them to meet her and make the offer.

"You helped protect my people and land. That above all else is what I ask of my princesses." The ruler smiled, a gentle thing that transformed an otherwise stern, sharp-angled face, a near-perfect match for her profile on the realm's coins.

"But I am Kitivan and I will never stop belonging there," Heron had said.

"I understand. Yet I make the offer all the same. Become one of my princesses and stay with us here in Codaros. You will find that we can give you things that your home does not. I will never ask you to choose between homes and peoples— only to do what you can for the well-being of all." She'd given them a few days to decide, but they'd left her knowing that she was right—that Codaros accepted them in ways Kitiva never had.

When they next saw her, they'd made promises to her, and

promises to home, and hadn't broken either no matter how much they bent them.

Yet.

Usually Heron enjoyed meandering through the gardens, whether following graveled paths or hard-packed earth. The warm, well-watered dirt supported an immense variety of trees and bushes, flowers and shrubs, in all colors. Glorious scents assaulted them wherever they turned.

This time, despite the equally lovely colors beginning to streak the sky, they paid no attention to their surroundings—only their destination . . . and whether or not anyone followed them.

All the while pretending they had nothing on their mind save an evening ramble in the growing shadows and chill as the sun reached the water.

Until they reached the arch in the stone wall that encircled the palace complex. Thick wooden doors reinforced with strips of metal lay ajar, offering a clear view through to the grove. Several trees grown wide with age formed a rough circle, with a graveled path leading around and through.

Guards in bright red tunics and mantles stood to either side of the gate. Each held a spear. One whistled a bawdy tune, stopping abruptly as Heron approached.

"Passing through?" One of the guards asked. The other leaned their spear against the wall, took up a tablet and stylus half-hidden in the shadows, and scrawled Heron's symbol.

"Sneaking in one last sunset at the point." Heron nodded.

"Should be a good one," the guard said, eyelids flickering. "You remember that the gate will be locked after the last light fades? No exceptions on reentering after, neither, not these days."

"I'll remember." Heron passed through and checked the sky. They'd arrived in time to watch the sunset and the colors, a good enough reason though they wondered if the guards suspected Heron met someone on the other side. A rendezvous perhaps?

If Heron remembered, it would be something to ask Emmi about in the morning.

Less gravel covered the path here, only a thin layer. The ground was just soft enough that every other step some of the gravel sunk down. Their calves ached from adjusting, but fortunately they didn't have to walk far—only around the grove to the far side where one person stood.

How had Stork arranged it? Might be fortune. Luck often favored Stork, given the hair-raising adventures he'd recounted over the years, apart from his regular meetings with Heron.

Looking at Stork gave Heron a sense of catching their future reflection in an almost-still puddle. A tall, thin man with a lanky form. Brown hair well-mixed with gray. Light wrinkles above high cheekbones adding character to a long, mobile face of light brown set with green-brown eyes.

Heron's own skin might be a step or two darker and their eyes solid brown, but there was no denying their relationship with their mother's youngest brother. They resembled each other even with Heron in the ankle-length tunic and layered mantle fashionable in Codaros while Stork wore a thigh-length blue vest over lightweight shirt and trousers that showed his thick leg muscles when the wind blew the right way. A heavy purse hung from his belt. His feet had to be sweating in ankle-high boots.

Having worn the same in their time as a trader, Heron preferred their current attire.

Stork crossed the few feet between them and grabbed Heron in a rib-creaking hug, happy as always to see them. Heron squeezed back, glorying in the warmth and pressure—but also moving so that the trees concealed the two of them from the guards.

"About time you got here, my boy." Stork let Heron go and gave them a warm pat on the back.

Heron gritted their teeth at the term that never fully fit them, but didn't offer a challenge or correction. Past experience offered painful reminders that pushing Stork to accept that Heron had no interest being a Kitivan man wasn't worth the trouble. Stork knew, he just didn't care. Regardless, he had no reticence in showing affection, and Heron had missed that. Codarans touched so infrequently—or at least touched *Heron* rarely.

Touch but little understanding or no touch and ample understanding. Unfortunately, Heron had yet to find a good balance in between.

"You're the one left this to the last minute," Heron said.

"The better to hide in all the hustle-bustle." Stork waved at the palace complex looming to the far sides of the trees. Despite the distance, many lights shone from the residential buildings as servants and others worked to prep the court for the usual split at the end of summer.

Heron pulled the folded parchment from their belt and handed the crackling packet over.

Stork unfolded the paper and squinted at it. "What's this?"

"Descriptions of the Dances done this summer, since the account of last year wasn't considered as helpful as could be. You're the one who told me that." Heron had carefully inscribed the Dances in as much detail as they could, given that movement was almost impossible to convey in words or words with sketches of how princesses and compeers moved around in circles, squares, or other forms.

"Eh." Stork leveled a stern glare at Heron. "You were asked for war dances."

He refolded the parchment and tucked it in his purse all the same.

"No one does war dances." Heron sighed, having said as much every time they met Stork. "The Terparchon's never so much as breathed a word about them in my presence."

"That doesn't matter. She may not be one to spill blood, but her heir will sure be. Been that way for generations. Nearly every other Terparchon conquers, and we must be ready." Stork gave Heron a reassuring shoulder squeeze. "So get them by the time we next meet, in Tharis this winter."

"I'm not even going with the Terparchon north, but with the Marchon on the southern circuit. If anyone knows war dances, surely it would be her." That assumed the Terparchon carried written descriptions of dances rather than having them in her head and visceral body memory. Heron could offer a dozen more arguments against the search, but Stork never followed him. The two might look alike, but the musicality and eagerness in the dance that filled Heron had completely skipped Stork.

"All the better. Get the information from him. He's got to know tricks with how he got the Terparchon to marry him despite being from the most recently conquered addition to Codaros." Stark shrugged, pointing at Heron. "And don't dally about, either. I'll be heading south and west myself before the end of fall, so I'll find you."

"What's the rush?" Heron pursed their lips, considering which objections Stork might actually listen to this time.

"You're almost at the five-year mark." Stork shook his head, drawing in a whistling breath as he studied Heron. "You'd know better than I how long princesses last in Codaros."

"Some dance ten years, twenty, or more." Alas, Heron could count the number of long-term princesses they knew on their hands. One decade-long princess they'd danced with earlier in the evening had showed signs of burning out.

"And many count themselves lucky to hang up their shoes after five or six." Stork clapped, making Heron start. "Might be you, so find the war dances and then get whatever parting gift you can out of the Terparchon and head on home where we'll be waiting with open arms. I've already had bids from two academies for your services as dance instructor, and there'll be more where those came from."

Heron loved their homeland. Loved their adopted country. Hated choosing between.

Hated having to.

"What if I don't go home after I retire?" Heron asked, skipping over the what if they didn't find the war dances, not having located any information yet.

"Why wouldn't you? Once a Kitivan always a Kitivan." Stork grimaced and poked a finger at Heron's chest. "Not that eleee nonsense again. The only true eleees are magic—and likely a fiction made up to fool folk into thinking they're something they're not."

Heron's hands clenched at their sides. They had to resist the challenge, because starting the argument—again—would only end in Heron being locked out of the palace complex and having to make their way around to the main entrance.

Unsatisfied, Stork tapped Heron's ears, nose, and shoulders. "Look at you, wearing long and looseys rather than a decent vest and trous. Surely you're ready to be a Kitivan again."

Such confidence, as though Stork thought they could read who Heron was inside from what they wore. Then again, for Stork and most Kitivans, the key to determining who a person was centered on their genitals.

Heron had come to a different understanding, but only after years of traveling through Codaros and other lands. The family had leased Heron out to the service of the council, in a similar if lesser fashion than Stork served, and unwittingly laid the groundwork for Heron realizing that not everyone divided people into two distinct and never-to-be-combined groups.

Heron couldn't go back to that.

But how could they stay in Codaros if they betrayed the trust extended to them here?

"We're counting on you." Stork grabbed Heron in a hug, gentler than the first.

Outside of dancing, no one had touched Heron since the last time they'd met Stork. They blinked away tears as they held their uncle close.

"I wasn't joking about Terparchons alternating between peace and war. Every other one." Stork pulled back, ruffling Heron's hair as he had when they were little. "Do your research, if you don't believe me and haven't already. And when the next Terparchon takes over, bent on conquest, where do you think she'll look? Up over the mountains or across the river at Kitiva? We don't want war. You know that. Neither do we want to be caught off guard. Find us directions on how to do war dances, sneak them out with no one the wiser, and your debt to the city will be paid."

"Truth?" Heron asked.

"Truth. Even if you decide to stay here. Though I'll come nag you about that if you do." Stork gave a last fond rub to Heron's head "You're my favorite nephew, even if you are the oddest of the lot."

Heron's head, shoulders and ribs ached from Stork's affection as they slipped back through the gates right before the guards locked up.

They trudged back through the gardens, taking as little notice of their surroundings as before, although this time partly due to the deepening shadows. They barely focused enough to take a different way than how they'd come, and found nothing to indicate anyone had followed them.

The Terparchon trusted them, and evidently so did the rest of the court, even if the courtiers didn't understand Heron any more than Heron understood their adopted home.

War dances. That was all the Kitivan council ever demanded of Heron since the surprise of becoming a princess in Codaros. The council didn't seem to care about all the reports of Dances that eased or banished storms, fires, floods, avalanches, earthquakes, pestilential fevers, and more that Heron had provided over the years. Ample material to give the sadly few Kitivan princesses ideas for Dances.

As they exited a stand of woods, they couldn't miss Emmi with her brother and daughter in the distance. The three were too far to approach, but easy to recognize all the same.

Merely seeing them made Heron long for their bed, a good night's sleep, and waking to the rattle of breakfast delivery and Emmi's cheery chatter.

Except the next morning, breakfast arrived without Emmi. Instead, a nervous young eleee barely old enough to decide whether or not they wanted to grow whiskers rolled in the tray and whispered they were newly appointed to care for Heron and their rooms. A child! All big brown eyes in a pale face and limbs still developing strength under their oversized tunic.

No Emmi.

Heron *had* missed something the evening before: Emmi saying goodbye.

Even if they tracked her down to apologize, they might never see her again except in passing.

Stork and the Kitivan council's desire for war dances had cost Heron a last evening's chat with the person in Codaros they liked best.

❧　5　❧

No matter that Emmi no longer attended a certain early-rising princess, she woke up at the usual hour.

Everything about the scene resembled the day before except the absence of any reason to rise just yet. The mattress filled most of the small room she shared with Susa, who always managed to wind up in the center by the end of the night. Emmi pulled her warm woolen blanket closer around her chin and kept the far ends tucked under her toes. The sweetgrass-stuffed pillow under her head could use a refresh, but she'd tend to that soon enough.

Everything in its place—a tricky balance to teaching a child, but Susa was learning. The predictability of Emmi's environs put her at ease.

Snores echoed through the thin walls, a regular reminder that not all attendants woke with the sun. Nor need Emmi. Desma had made it clear she might rest and report a little later.

A spider wove a web in the far corner of the ceiling that sparkled in the first angled rays of sunlight passing through the narrow window. Emmi would remove the spider before heading off to work. No sense in accepting in her own room an untidiness she cleared up in others.

She might give it to Susa and see if the girl could carry the creature outside without squashing it.

Or perhaps not yet.

Susa lay curled into a ball in her own blanket, a grouchy ball that had pried three stories from her uncle-aunt the night before and didn't want to wake. Emmi had to nudge her three times before she rubbed her eyes and roused enough to get up.

Then Susa refused to clean her face with the water Emmi had lugged up. Too chilly, from having sat out all night in the pitcher. Emmi dipped her fingers and flicked drops at Susa, and then accepted an otherwise lost battle.

The day turned worse when Susa decided she didn't want to get dressed. She lay limp, declining to fight as Emmi prodded and pulled at her daughter's limbs. Emmi gave up on neatness or tidiness, as the lovely clean light-blue tunic showed a myriad of wrinkles after being pulled over Susa's head. Susa sat up just enough to let Emmi fasten the sash around her waist. Both would turn grayish and spotted by the end of the day, but one of the benefits of working for the palace was handing their dirty clothes to the launderers once a week.

Little though Emmi wanted, she donned her nicest work clothes: a scrupulously clean gray tunic under a new solid yellow mantle with the court's insignia embroidered in green. Someone had left the mantle in a wrapped package on Emmi's doorstep the afternoon before, likely at Desma's behest. Under the circumstances, Emmi dug into the cranny where she hid her few valuables and hung delicate copper hoops from her ears.

The day got a bit better when Susa nibbled on a day-old savory redberry pastry Aurel had provided, in the end consuming even the scorched corner that had rendered it unsuitable for others in the court. Emmi took advantage of the child's distraction to roll up the mattress and pillows and tuck them in a corner near the wicker baskets that held most of their worldly belongings.

The next moment, despite donning her sandals, Susa whined about walking over to the children's palace—a tall stone edifice surrounded by stone walls and mixed grass-and-mud playing fields—for lessons and play. Again, she didn't resist Emmi guiding her and nudging her down the stairs and on the way.

Perhaps Susa had picked up on Emmi's reluctance to start her new assignment, or come up with a bad day on her own, but getting her on her way at least kept Emmi too busy to fret.

Much.

Emmi turned her daughter over to the usual early morning attendant at the children's palace, and headed into the kitchens. She paused long enough in Aurel's domain to give him a quick hug and get another in return, plus a fresher pastry to munch on.

But she could only put off for so long meeting Desma in the supply warren.

The older woman wore her usual layers of yellow, mantle wrapped tight against the morning chill as she waited for Emmi to check over and assemble an array of cleaning supplies: cloths, brushes, buckets . . . scented cleaning powders.

"Not the lavender," Desma coughed as Emmi reached for her usual allotment. "The sonnewood."

"Truly?" Emmi opened the sonnewood bin and shuddered at the heavy, smoky scent. Grabbing the dipper, she half-filled a small clamshell box.

"Zora prefers sonnewood in her rooms, but otherwise disdains perfume." Desma shrugged. "Her clothes are not to be dusted with scent during laundering."

"I presume the launderers are well aware." Emmi loaded the supplies on a small wagon. "What else?"

"No food in the morning, as she doesn't break her fast until midday. Doesn't wake until the first court bell rings, either, at which time she'll want a large pitcher of warm water for washing and a smaller of plain with no more and no less than five pieces of ice."

"Does she count?" Emmi muttered under her breath as she picked out two appropriate-sized pitchers started dragging the wagon, but of course Desma heard. They were alone in the room, the attendants serving early risers having been and gone and the later crew yet to show.

"I wouldn't dare guess."

Meaning Emmi shouldn't test the matter.

She followed Desma across the largest plaza in the service area, with its simple mosaic of stars formed from black and white stones. Down one passageway and across a second, smaller plaza decorated in seashells lay the central well house, one of the five that kept the palace supplied with drinkable water. The straw-lined back room held the precious, dwindling stock of ice.

The particularity of Zora's requirements, so different from the easy-going Heron, Gisela, and Jola, set Emmi's nerves jangling.

Perhaps the princesses were particular too, in their own ways, or so Emmi tried to assure herself. She found no comfort in the thought. If they were, Emmi had learned their likes and dislikes to the point she could predict with a high degree of accuracy whether or not they'd like new things—scents, foods, clothes. True, she'd only started serving Gisela a few moons earlier, but certain things were common across princesses.

Zora was a compeer, one of the people trained to partner princesses and ensure they made the most of their magic. Also a dancer, but also the daughter of Codaros's rulers.

Emmi was starting all over and would have to figure out what Zora needed versus what she wanted versus what was feasible.

The actual introduction proved in keeping with the rest of the morning.

Desma tapped lightly on the door while Emmi allowed herself this once to gape at her surroundings.

She'd rarely been in the lower levels of the heart of the palace complex, and never up to the hall where the royal family had their chambers. Everything was wider, taller than the princesses' quarters, not fancier as both boasted intricate mosaics on the floors and walls. Yet the mosaics in the princesses' hall were purely decorative—seascapes, starry expanses, rolling hills.

Here the mosaics portrayed past Terparchons and the many battles and negotiations that had built Codaros from one city to a powerful land encompassing many cities and peoples.

Both royal and princess halls had four small-wheeled carts to use to move food, drink, and cleaning supplies around the floor, once one had hauled them up the back stairs or hefted the ropes to bring them up on the narrow lifting platform built into the stairwell.

Four for four royal suites, rather than four shared across a dozen princesses. That, at least, would make Emmi's life a little easier.

From the breadth of hall, Emmi could guess at the size of the rooms she'd be tending: twice as big as any of the princesses, and with large windows overlooking the lake.

The first bell rang out, vibrations rippling through the walls and floor. Desma had timed their arrival almost to the minute.

Desma tapped again.

No answer on the other side of the door, or any sounds indicating Zora had risen.

Desma knocked, louder.

"Go away!" Zora said, clearly a snarl despite the muffled quality.

Desma grimaced, then wiped the scowl off her face.

"Wait." Zora said, almost as harsh but several tones higher.

The pitter patter of footsteps drew closer, then the door was wrenched open.

Emmi had seen Zora many times over the years, always from a respectful distance. The royal compeer never appeared anything but sleek and well-kept even when leaving the dancing pavilion in the middle of the night after a Dance.

A very different figure stood on the other side of the doorway: short and slight with dark brown hair pulled back in a thick braid from which some strands had escaped to make a wispy effect. Matching dark brown eyes fixed on Desma; they were set in an oval face with a sharp nose and thin lips pressed tight together.

The compeer hadn't put anything on her feet and wore a thread-bare sleep tunic as plain as Susa's. She stood a few inches taller than Emmi's daughter. Enough shorter than Emmi to give a good view at where Zora's tunic had slipped down on one shoulder showing faint bruises and scratches on the front and top but not the back. Finger-marks, but at such an angle Emmi couldn't guess how anyone had created them, unless perhaps Zora had tried to pick up a resisting child?

Before Emmi could spiral into speculation, Zora glanced at her.

The royal blinked several times, the expression in her eyes shifting with each, then turned back to Desma.

"You have another candidate?" Both eyebrows rose high.

"The last you'll need." Desma nodded. "May I present Emmi? She's served at court for over a decade and cared for several princesses single-handedly for the last five years. I'm sure she'll suffice."

"That's what you said last time." Zora leaned against the side of the doorway, arms crossed over her chest.

"And did the last candidate not meet your needs?" Desma asked.

Zora paused and pursed her lips, then she jerked her head to the side. "Yes, they were satisfactory. Barely."

"Unfortunately, they could not say the same," Desma said. "They found you . . . unpredictable, unnerving even."

Emmi sucked in her breath, amazed that Desma spoke so plainly.

"I hope you will be less so with Emmi." Desma smiled and extended her hands in the directions of compeer and new attendant.

Zora drew in a deep breath. Her throat tightened as she swallowed hard. Expression tired, she turned to meet Emmi's gaze. "*I'll* try."

Emmi noted the emphasis on the first word. At least one of the selves, number still unclear, had agreed to do their best. She could ask for more, but would take what she was given. "If you'll be so kind as to let me know your preferences, I'll do my best to please."

Zora reared, stepping backward, then laughed and smiled. Glancing at Desma, Zora asked "What did you do, make her drink a full pitcher of sugared water before bringing her up?" Without waiting for response, she turned her attention back to Emmi. "Here are the most important rules. Put everything back where you found it. Never take anything away without checking first, except the dirty laundry. And never, ever touch me, no matter what."

The first stricture was music to Emmi's heart—things tidy and in their place. The second seemed commonsense. Nevertheless, a creeping sensation rolled up Emmi's spine. "I'll do my best."

Zora opened the door wider and let Emmi in with her cart of supplies. Desma slipped away with only a brief glance back.

Within a few moments, Emmi had a good guess as to how many individuals resided inside Zora. She couldn't imagine how Desma missed it, unless Desma deliberately didn't say or had never actually been in Zora's rooms, for the room was clearly divided into four unequal parts.

Closest to the door was a section set up as a reception area with two couches and a small table. It resembled the princesses' smaller outer rooms, and showed signs of regular use and needing cleaning, but no more than anything left untended for a few days. The couches had a glorious view of the lake—but were marred by odd marks and strange oval divots in the cushions bearing halos of creamy hair.

Restoring it all to clean, orderly condition would be a pleasure.

Alas, nearby rested a third couch piled with clothes, trinkets, and what might be the ends of scrolls and books amidst the mess. Did Zora intend Emmi to maintain the piles in their current order? Mere proximity to the disorder made her shudder.

In sharp contrast, a series of shelves beyond were kept scrupulously in order and tidy, a relief. They bore an array of locked boxes and wicker baskets. The metal trim on the boxes shone, and the wicker appeared to have been dusted recently, likely by the wadded tunic thrown atop the messy couch given the dust marks on the otherwise still good fabric.

Lastly, the interior wall bore a long, detailed mosaic of a former Terparchon—Emmi wasn't certain which—extending an open hand and clutching a sword and scroll in the other. A small section of the floor near the base of the tiled figure was set off by a semi-circle of tiles laid atop the wooden floor. The tiles had come from the wall, chipped out of the Terparchon's outstretched hand.

Yet whatever tool Zora had used to loosen the mortar and free the tiles was nowhere in sight. Unless she'd used her fingernails, which at a glance appeared short and uneven.

Then the cat strode through the archway from the bedchamber, furry paws stomping straight across the loose tiles with disturbing a single one. Its sleek coat was a cream color tipped with silver-gray, and the lashing tail striped in dark gray. A long pink tongue swiped over sharp teeth, then it leapt onto the overloaded couch and settled atop the dusty tunic.

A cat.

The previous Terparchon, whom Emmi had only ever seen from a distance a few times when she first started working at court, disdained animals save for oxen who pulled the wagons when the court went on progress—or the army to war. The old woman mostly ignored dogs so long as they remained on the outskirts of court and didn't leave any smelly signs of their existence where she walked—but she'd reportedly particularly detested cats.

Habits died hard. Even a decade after the former ruler's death, very few people at court kept pets. The overseers of supplies in Yaras and Tharis used cats to avoid pest invasions but made sure the animals never ventured far from the storerooms. Some people who stayed in the palaces year-round had small dogs, who were kept at the outskirts.

Emmi had no pets, though she'd grown up with barn cats who paid little mind to her once they grew past kitten-hood. She knew of no one who went on progress, whether courtier or attendant, possessed of a pet.

Certainly not Zora's parents.

Yet the cat appeared quite comfortable in Zora's rooms. The compeer smiled at it and sneered in the same moment. Emmi edged closer to the door, and farther from the creature.

She was no longer puzzled by number of staff who'd declined to work for Zora, and not sure how long she would last.

Neither had she any idea which Zora she was working for at the moment, except whoever gazed out of Zora's eyes appeared less grouchy and more tired than Susa.

Royal compeer she might be, but she was perhaps half Emmi's age. Emmi had promised to try.

But oh how she wished she was still serving Heron.

6

Heron missed Emmi.

Every movement of their new attendant stood in sharp contrast to Emmi's ease, familiarity, and comfort. Fotis, the eleee who'd stumbled over sharing their name in a whisper, glanced over at Heron between every task, nearly between every breath. In the past, except when called for an early dance practice, Heron had often lingered in their rooms while Emmi cleaned, enjoying the give and take of conversation and Emmi's insights into dealing with the Codaros court.

The contrast drove Heron away.

They dressed in attire suitable for practice—plain tunic and mantle, sandals with solid soles—and fled. Down the hall they strode with long steps, noting but ignoring the sounds of movement in other princesses' quarters. Their stomach complained, as they'd barely nibbled on their breakfast because their vegetable rolls and pastry simultaneously tasted the same as always and as though made of ashes.

Within moments, they descended the stairs and crossed from the residence to the dancing pavilion. Only two startled attendants were there, one cleaning the entry hall floor and the other carrying piles of clean linens into the bathing areas.

Heron nodded at them and proceeded to the central chamber, the practice room. Two stories high, it had seven windows inset in the roof that allowed in light all day long. Brass lanterns along the wood panel walls provided illumination at night. A balcony ringed the second floor, allowing the Terparchon or her chosen substitutes to oversee the dancing from above if they chose.

The floor bore an intricate image of done in paint on wood, and retouched every winter no doubt as it always appeared fresh at the start of the summer and somewhat scratched and marred by the end. The mix of natural elements—shells, stars, flames, waves, and more—seemed to move when glanced at out of the corner of one's eye.

Heron paused several steps in to breathe deep. Despite the best efforts of the servants, the tang of sweat always undergirded whatever cleaning solution they applied. The scent alone affirmed Heron stood in a place they didn't associate with Emmi.

With no one else around, they went through their usual morning stretches. First a course of salutations to the sun, stretching their arms and legs. Next invocations of sowing and reaping, foraging and harvesting, working their midsection and remembering the importance of ensuring daily bread. Last, floor exercises reconnecting with earth, albeit through the wood floor, for from earth humans came and to earth they would return.

When another princess or the Terparchon's substitute made them stretch before dancing, Heron followed whatever they requested. Bits that they'd learned over the years had crept into their usual routine, but the core remained the same.

The cycle of Kitivan exercises led readily into a line dance. If Heron closed their eyes, they could pretend they were back in the city during one of the two major festivals—spring or autumn. The streets filled with dancers in lines, men north or east and women south or west, sometimes for a mile or more. Pairs performed matching steps, regularly meeting to whirl in the middle and shift position. Sometimes they'd change partners in the process. If one wanted, one could dance from sunup to sundown.

Step to the right, back to the left.

Clap twice.

Step in to clap one's partner's hands.
Step back.
Step in, arms around waists, lean back, and whirl.

So easy to imagine being back in the hustle and bustle, with musicians playing variations of the same songs in different keys and measures. People singing and mangling lyrics that no one could hear anyway. Anyone who couldn't abide disharmony fled Kitiva at the festivals.

But it was a glorious cacophony, made more wonderful in imagination with Emmi dancing opposite.

Heron stumbled to a halt. They pressed a fist against their chest, trying to squash down the guilt rising up their throat.

For not having realized Emmi was saying goodbye, because Heron was too busy worrying about being caught between allegiances.

For Kitiva, because Stork was right. Given Codaros's history, the current Terparchon might be peaceful, and her heir possibly the same, but sooner than later a ruler of Codaros would set out to conquer more territories, and Heron didn't want Kitiva added to Codaros, no matter how much they liked both.

Heron didn't know what to do about any of it.

So they sought refuge in the remembered line dance. This time, they kept their eyes open, the better to not picture Emmi opposite them.

A fortunate decision, because with no more warning than a few squeaky footsteps across the wood floor, a dancer joined them. Another princess took up a place across from Heron. Gisela, the newest princess, from some speck on the map near where the court sometimes passed on progress.

Dark curls flying around her round face, her pink tunic flared and sandals scraped the floor. She tried to fit her movements to Heron's, but her steps weren't quite the same. She moved to the wrong side half the time, snapped her fingers instead of clapping, and whirled more than Heron so that they wound up smacking into each other and falling to the floor.

Heron rolled to the side, wincing as they extracted their knee and calf from under Gisela's legs. This was the only kind of touch in their life these days—on the dance floor, or by accident, or both.

Applause sounded from near the door.

Amara stood there, a broad smile stretching her lilac-colored skin. Her white hair hung low in a thick braid over her blue mantle and tunic. As the oldest retired princess still at court, she sometimes stood in for the Terparchon.

Gisela laughed as she clambered to her feet. "That was fun. Until it wasn't. What were you dancing?"

"A line dance." Heron sat with their feet straight ahead as they stretched their arms. A crick in their back eased. "The kind of thing sometimes done by dozens, hundreds, in the streets of Kitiva."

"Hmm, we do similar things in Foleilion." Gisela grimaced as she flexed her back. "But evidently not quite similar enough."

"It was a nice try." Amara came closer, her sandals making little more than a whisper on the wood. "Perhaps we should practice some line dances for use in Dancing, or for a demonstration at the next Court ball."

"On the progress or once we're back in Tharis for the winter?" Heron asked. With any luck, the notion would vanish never to reappear.

"Good question, I'll have to think about it," Amara said.

Gisela peered down at Heron. "Are you all right?

"I'm no more hurt than at any practice, other than my dignity." Heron leapt to their feet.

"That's not what I meant." Gisela shook her head. "When we came in and first saw you dancing, you looked so sad, as if the bottom fell out of your world."

Heron opened their mouth to pass it off, then paused. Glanced back and forth between Gisela and Amara. Such very different people, one the quintessential courtier and the other still new and shiny. Usually Heron kept their questions for Emmi, but they couldn't any longer, especially this one.

They'd never had to apologize at such a level here before. "Let's say there's someone . . . what's a good way in Codaros to say I'm sorry? In

Kitiva, we'd bribe a friend to sing a song outside the person's house. Or send an official apologizer."

Heron got more advice than they'd expected or could use, but that was why, late in the afternoon, they followed a twisty path through the palace to a part they'd rarely visited.

The children's palace.

The building itself was unremarkable, just one of the many multi-storied stone edifices in the complex. It sat on the north side, protected by high walls and an inlet of the lake reputedly filled with sharp rocks fit to puncture any boat or swimmer.

A rectangular plaza with several benches and bushes in planters offered seating near the passageways leading to the rest of the complex, but most of the plaza had been turned into a walled-in area filled with children running, screaming, digging in piles of earth, swinging on ropes hung from a tall, sturdy tree. Several older attendants watched over the children but did nothing to reduce the cries, yells, and thuds echoing back from the surrounding walls.

Heron stayed well back from the low wall edging the play area. After inspecting the narrow plaza, they settled onto a bench in a far corner, out of the sun and partly hidden by a large, leafy bush.

Each and every one of the children was spotted with dirt and streaked with sweat. Even the attendants looked decidedly unkempt no matter how nice they might have dressed in the morning.

Better that Heron stay in the shadow, for they'd donned a favorite tunic of light green and delicately draped mantle of darker green edged in twined silver and gold, matching trim on their sandals. Emmi had praised the outfit earlier in the summer, saying the green brought out lovely gold undertones in their skin.

Fingers twitching, they settled the basket they'd carefully carried at their side. They'd gone through enough trouble for the contents to take care.

Big apologies in Codaros evidently required a gift, a physical representation of their regret—but not just any gift.

Gisela warned them to consider carefully what they wanted out of the apology and match the gift to that.

At which Amara had said that if they wanted more, then they

should choose something that showed how well they knew the person's likes and dislikes.

Emmi's name hadn't entered into the discussion at any point, but Heron suspected one or both had guessed. It all sounded as though apologizing was a half-step toward courting.

Regardless, Heron had taken the advice and ordered a special batch of lavender-starmeg pastries from Emmi's sibling. The pastries were a recipe from Emmi's home, something she'd once mentioned missing.

Heron wouldn't mind if they never had to meet up with Aurel again. Emmi's brother had been perfectly polite, perhaps because there were a lot of other cooks around and potentially listening to Heron's request, but he'd glared at Heron the whole time. When he handed over the triangular pastries, pink and oozing with sweet cream, he'd carefully deposited them in the basket and covered with a dainty blue cloth—then shoved the basket into Heron's belly.

"I'm doing this because *she* likes them," Aurel had said. "Not because *you* asked." Then he'd blinked and given Heron a cold once-over and turned away.

If the pastries were meant for Heron, they'd worry about Aurel slipping in ingredients that would make them sick.

Now they just had to wait for Emmi to come pick up her daughter.

The people overseeing the children noticed Heron's presence, but evidently recognized them and that they were waiting. They got a couple of smiles and nods, but nothing more.

Most of the parents coming to retrieve their children didn't seem to notice, as Heron remained in the shadow, hidden by the plant.

The number of children dwindled until only three handfuls remained, including Emmi's daughter. Heron noticed her right off, from the few times they interacted.

They were relieved that Susa was having fun and didn't notice when Emmi hustled through archway leading from the children's palace to the central hall and royal dwellings. A few strands of her hair stuck to her forehead, and her tunic and mantle had distinct wrinkle marks on either side exactly where she might grip tight.

Otherwise she was the same, just no longer Heron's attendant.

They chose their spot perfectly, because she had to pass close to reach the gate to fetch her daughter.

"Emmi."

She stopped. Her back stiffened. She turned her head, shoulders facing away. "What are you doing here?"

"I wanted . . ." Heron rose, picked up the basket, and moved closer, leaving only an arm's length between them. "I'm sorry."

"Sorry for what?" She didn't move or turn any further.

"I didn't know yesterday was the end until too late."

"I told you." This time, she turned around, although not all the way. She ran a shaky hand through her hair, face lined with exhaustion.

"I know, I wasn't listening. I'm sorry. I just wanted to be sure you knew that having you around since I became a princess, all the advice you gave me, all the times you listened. It means a lot." Heron held out the basket.

Emmi stiffened, then her nose twitched. Her eyes grew wide. She sniffed and then grasped the basket gingerly, pulling aside the cloth covering and staring down at the triangular pastries. A soft, incredulous smile filled her face with light. "These are my favorite."

"I know."

"How?"

"You told me."

"I mentioned it maybe once?" She lifted the basket up and practically stuck her face in. When she pulled back, surprise had wiped some of the tiredness from her face. "Did you get these from Aurel?"

"You said no one else in Yaras makes them half as well as him." Heron shrugged.

"And he made them for you?"

"No, he made them for *you*." Heron smiled. "Even though I was the one who asked for them."

"That sounds like him." Emmi said.

"And I asked because I'm sorry. If I'd listened last night, we could've . . . I could've . . ." Heron shrugged again, too aware that they'd had the meeting with Stork hanging over their head. "I miss you already."

"It would've been easier to stay taking care of you," Emmi said.

"And Gisela and Jola, but Desma asked me to make the change and I couldn't say no. I'll miss you, too."

Her words eased Heron's guilt but did nothing to stop the ache of knowing they'd not see her again day-in, day-out. But they had no reason to stay except drinking in these last moments close to her, and she had to get her daughter.

"Enjoy the pastries." Heron nodded at Susa, still playing in the distance. "Don't let your daughter eat them all."

"I won't."

With her promise ringing in their ears, Heron turned to go.

Only to have Emmi reach for them. "Wait." Her fingers rested on their upper arm.

Heron's mouth gaped. They turned their head only and stared at her, frozen and hot at the same moment because she touched them. The first time, skin to skin.

They'd rarely seen people at court touch each other, save between relatives or lovers. So different from the casual touches in Kitiva, all the hugs and taps and pats on the cheek. Shook hands on meeting, rather than nodded and bowed.

They hadn't realized how much they'd missed contact.

Yet Emmi had touched Heron. She'd reached out and laid warm fingers on their forearm, though she seemed startled at her own action.

"You put thought into your apology. Brought me something you believed I'd like and were right." Emmi ducked her head. "Thank you."

Without conscious thought, Heron shifted to hold her fingers in theirs. They faced her, met her gaze straight on. Moving slowly, clasp loose enough that she could pull away at any moment, they lifted her hand to their lips and brushed her skin.

Her chest heaved and she shivered, a hint of incredulous smile on lips.

Heron likewise struggled for breath, whole being focused on the points where skin met skin.

She'd touched them first. She'd reached out.

They'd responded.

Emmi no longer attended them. The gulf of power between them had lessened. Letting go of her hand, Heron waited for her to take the next step.

Her lips parted, but Susa shrieked, "Mama!"

"Just a moment!" Emmi called to her daughter. She held the hand Heron had kissed against their chest. "Another time?" she asked Heron.

They nodded, smiled, and slipped away full of new, unformed hope.

All the while cradling the arm she'd touched and hand that had caressed her.

7

"I loved your pastries." Emmi hugged Aurel.

She settled onto an uneven three-legged stool that shifted until she decided which way to rest her weight. Her skin turned slick with perspiration despite her trip to the baths after a morning scrubbing Zora's washroom from top to bottom. Her second-worst tunic started to stick to her skin, her worst tunic now residing in the laundry pile. Her hair had yet to dry, damp strands lying limp along the sides of her head.

The long kitchen had plenty of high windows on either side, carefully opened to catch whatever drafts they could. The walls were plaster and whitewash over stone, unfortunately retaining a fair amount of heat. A line of baking ovens stretched across the near wall, no longer in use and the ashes raked out of the fire pits. Fires continued to burn at the far end, beyond row after row of wooden tables bearing all manner of cooking implements, while copper pots and pans hung along the walls and from the rafters, providing decoration and reflecting light from the windows and lanterns.

The cook fires generated so much heat that the draft did little good. The cooks watching the pots had all slipped the tunics off their shoulders to pool at their waists. Sweaty backs and chests marked the two male cooks, one female, and an eleee, all busy chopping vegetables and watching over bubbling pots. Barley soup, something with lemon, and something else with honey vinegar, but they all smelled good.

Aural hadn't undone his tunic during his labors, given the flour, fruit sauces, and mashed greens streaking the light green fabric. More flour matted his hair where he'd grabbed it at some point, for the mark was roughly in the shape of a handprint. His face and hands were scrupulously clean as he put a low, narrow table in front of Emmi and then topped it with a platter of thin breads, vegetables, and cheese and onion dip. Bustling around, he added a pitcher of well-watered wine, or water flavored with light grape seasoning, and two chipped goblets. At last he settled down opposite her, his stool rocking almost as badly as hers.

"I'm delighted the pastries pleased," he finally said, though he sounded more grumpy than glad.

The gloominess suggested she faced Aurel. Rellie tended to get whiny when out of sorts rather than dour, while Auri went quiet and snapped at anyone who disturbed her.

"I made them for *you*," he added after a long pause.

"So Heron said." She spread the dip on a finger of bread and nearly moaned at the glorious taste.

"Good." He gave an odd noise, half-laughter and half-grunt. "I didn't think they would, after coming down here and asking for me and only me to cook for them."

"The sweets were a gift when they apologized to me." Emmi followed the cheese with a sip of water, finding it cooler than expected. Condensation on the pitcher meant Aurel had snuck a few pieces of ice for them.

"That's done then, and you won't see them much anymore." He dug into the vegetables, crunching on a stick of blanched carrot.

"Aren't you even curious why they apologized?" She jerked as one of the cooks at the far end banged a metal spoon against the side of a boiling pot. Aurel hardly flinched.

"Whatever it was for, it wasn't for the right things." Another crunched carrot. "They should've apologized long ago for keeping you dangling around making things nice and sweet and easy for them."

"That's harsh." She sat back, unbalancing the stool legs, and quickly leaned her weight forward again.

"I've seen how they watched you when they thought no one was looking. Time after time, but they did nothing, said nothing, for years!"

Emmi wrapped her hands around the still-cool goblet and drank deep. Aurel's sentiments hadn't changed. He'd said the same often enough, never realizing that it always gave Emmi a secret thrill to know someone else had spotted a glint of interest in Heron's gaze. That it wasn't Emmi's imagination.

"I worked for them, and you know the rule: don't mess with anyone over whom you have power," Emmi said, snagging the last carrot before Aurel could gnash on it as well. "I reported to Desma, and Janida before her, but I worked for Heron and Jola and—"

"The rules aren't the same for them, for the folks up top,"—he pointed his little finger at the floors above, as if his words didn't suffice —"as for us. If Heron really wanted to be with you, they could've asked for you to be reassigned. It mightn't've been easy, but they could've managed it, and then even though you'd have figured out it wouldn't work between you sooner than later, you'd at least have had some moments of bliss out of all your labors."

Easing the stool to rest on a different pair of legs, Emmi studied her brother. Despite dwelling on Heron—and sneaking yet his usual references to her lack of a love life—Aurel appeared distracted. His shoulders slumped, lips curved down, and on closer glance the treats he'd brought for them to share were all his favorites.

Exactly what he usually consumed when crossed in love.

She hadn't seen Aurel flirting with anyone recently, but he always had been secretive about his loves after being burned once too often on flings in his youth.

"Who is it?" Emmi asked.

"None of your business." He spread cheese and onions on bread so energetically it nearly tore in half, leaving cheese smeared across his fingers.

Instant denial rather than puzzlement, which meant she was on the right path. She leaned over and squeezed his hand, ignoring the cheese dip that smeared onto her skin.

He squeezed back, head low.

An exchange of unspoken sympathy, and yet it reminded Emmi of touching Heron, and them kissing her hand.

Aurel's grouchiness might be over his own love life, but he had a point about Emmi and Heron. Either could have asked for her to be reassigned so they might explore the possibilities between them.

Neither had.

The matter followed her throughout the day, recurring anytime she paused or took a rest between labors.

Zora had returned to her room and taken to her bed for a nap. Fortunately the cat stayed with her. Her presence required Emmi clean quietly. So she worked on the uncluttered couches, scrubbing the frames before tackling the cushions.

The sonnewood-scented cleaning powder quickly vanquished any hint of animal stench—but many of the hairs had worked into the tight-woven fabric. She changed the angle of the cleaning cloth regularly, teasing out orange-tipped cream hair after hair.

Hands busy, but mind wandering free to wonder why she'd let the situation with Heron go on for years.

She'd been a young mother when she first met Heron, distracted caring for an active toddler and unwilling to admit attraction to a princess in her care—and still sore over the embers of the once-blazing love she'd shared, or thought she shared, with Susa's father. Whom Emmi dealt with well enough now, time having granted perspective.

When Susa's father apologized—which he'd had to do so often Emmi sometimes wondered if he enjoyed messiness as much as she abhorred it—he'd always brought something he enjoyed as a gift. His favorite sweets, his favorite flowers.

Never *her* beloved lavender-starmeg pastries.

After the first year or two tending Heron, Emmi began to suspect her partiality. Even when she was no longer able to deny it to herself she remained unsure that the attraction was mutual. Why risk disrupting things for nothing? It was so comforting to be able to talk to Heron over the years, exchanging stories of Codaros and Kitiva. Feeling special at being able to explain to them why courtiers did this or that. Enjoying how they always inquired about her life and Susa's latest antics.

The more time passed, the more she valued what she had and feared the risk of losing it. Especially since she wasn't always sure that Heron wanted more.

Among the tales of attendants falling in love with the people they cared for were ample comic and tragic instances where the objects turned out to have no interest in the servant. In the best stories, the servant was lucky to lose love or position—or both. The sadder tales ended in death, suicide or murder.

She shook her head as she patted the cushions back into shape and replaced them on the frame.

A moment later, Zora woke long enough to scream at the cat to get out.

The cat, that was one indicator of which Zora was in control. The main Zora cuddled the beast, calling it Sweetie and Snookums even though she'd named it Homer.

Homer strolled out from the bedchamber, at first hastily then at more leisure as Zora slammed the door shut between the rooms. Sauntering over to check out Emmi's labor, it leapt onto the couch and curled up right on the spot she'd spent the most time on scrubbing clean.

Emmi flinched, sighed, and left the couch to the cat. Checking the angle of the sun, she made a trip down to the far end of the hall to fetch fresh drinking and wash water, then decided to cease labors for the afternoon.

Leave the royal compeer to her sleep. Zora would likely have Emmi working extra hours in the next few days, packing wooden trunks for the progress. Zora's trunks. Fortunately, the water-proof leaves affixed to the sides easily took paint. Every trunk bore some kind of decoration clearly distinguishing one from another. All of Zora's had some combination of purple strikes and gold circles.

Dragging cleaning supplies down to the warren, Emmi paused as one of the working cats slipped down the hall. Its tail flicked as it turned a corner and went on its merry way. She sighed, finding cats much easier to face and deal with down in the shared spaces rather than in someone's personal rooms.

A pet. Something Emmi vowed never to mention to Susa, in case her daughter decided they needed one.

She picked up a message from a fellow attendant. Welcoming a reason to leave, she hurried over to the top floor of the building where the princesses lived. She'd climbed the stairs to the princesses' floor so many times she paused and nearly stopped rather than continuing on up.

Her progress slowed to a trudge as she rose higher, into warmer air. At the top she took the time to brush wrinkles and smudges from her tunic and wipe sweat from her brow. Might as well present the best version of herself she could, given she'd cleaned most of the day.

No sooner had Emmi knocked on the door at the far end of the corridor than it opened to reveal Amara on the other side rather than her attendant. Her deep purple tunic brought out the odd silvery undertones to her lilac skin.

"Good, you got my message promptly," the retired princess said.

"I'm at your disposal." Emmi gave a slight bow.

"I only ask a little conversation on a matter or two that may be of use to you." Amara opened the door wide.

Emmi blinked, unsure how to take the words, but lacked any reason not to enter.

Amara's chambers had the same basic layout as the princesses' below. Two couches, with cushions in dark blue and pale yellow—and not a single cat hair in sight—sat at angles near the window with a low table between. A pitcher of water and two goblets rested on the table. Either they were scented or Amara favored a lemony perfume given the hint of citrus in the air.

The mosaics on floor and walls portrayed stars and starry nights— deep blues speckled with pointed spots of yellow and silver, while an immense white moon practically glowed from the wall opposite the window. The room faced away from the lake, with a view of the great square and the front gates in the distance. Perhaps it was bright in the morning, but even with a lantern glowing from the center of the moon, it was dim in the afternoon.

"Please,"—Amara waved at the couches—"sit, and may I offer you something to drink?"

Emmi settled nervously on the couch, letting her feet dangle off the side rather than set dusty sandals on the clean fabric. The frame was sturdy, but one of the cushions sighed under her weight.

Amara reclined on other couch, gracing Emmi with a polite smile. "How are things going with Zora?"

Back stiffening, Emmi swallowed and stroked away a stray cat hair spotted on her tunic.

Why had Amara summoned Emmi—for her own reasons, or for the Terparchon's? Attendants sometimes referred to Amara in whispers as the Terparchon's shadow, doing whatever the ruler asked, whether the kind of action suitable for bright day or deepest nights. Although Amara might ask out of her own interest, a wise person assumed that Amara would feel free to share whatever she knew with the Terparchon.

Emmi wouldn't speak out of turn anyway. Complaints should go up the proper chain of command except when that failed. Not that she'd complained or planned to anytime soon.

"I'm honored with the trust of looking after Zora," Emmi said.

"And that's all you're going to tell me." Amara nodded. "Very well. I understand. There are many things I cannot share for tradition, kindness, or other reasons. Still, there are matters I *can* speak about, and you can listen, even if you do not open your mouth."

Emmi picked up the goblet Amara had offered her, wrapping her hands around it as a way to keep her fingers from twitching. One of the benefits of working for princesses was that she hadn't received much attention from the upper levels of the court. Zora was evidently a different matter.

"You may hear people say that Zora has always been difficult." Amara shook her head. "That's not true. I, for one, can pinpoint the day and time that things changed, but that has no relevance here. It doesn't change the challenge you have before you." She leaned forward, voice dropping. "What you need to know is that the Terparchon appointed her elder daughter to remain behind when the court splits, to stand in the Terparchon's stead and welcome envoys while the rest of us go on the usual progress south and north."

Hardly news to Emmi. Everyone had talked about it since the announcement the night before.

"This may be a disappointment for Zora. There are those who thought she might be named instead."

Amara's pause allowed Emmi to work through the implications. Those who thought, perhaps including Zora herself? It would explain Zora's retreat to her bedroom and ill temper. "Thank you for the information, it is timely."

"You've met Homer by now." Amara sat back, intertwining her fingers.

"Yes." Emmi shivered.

"Watch Homer—make friends with him if you can. No one knows her moods as well as him. If the cat ever runs from her, that's when you need to be the most wary." Amara grimaced and reached for her goblet drinking deep. "Even run away yourself. Find me if you can, but get away."

Valuable as the information was, Emmi squirmed. It was unsettling in too many ways, not least the suggestion that Emmi might be in danger, and Zora a source of harm—and that Emmi should be ready to run from Zora's rooms.

Her discomfort may have shown on her face, for Amara raised a hand and nodded.

"We'll leave it at that for now, but if you ever desire assistance or advice," Amara said, "please do not hesitate to come to me."

"I appreciate the offer." Emmi moved to rise, but subsided when Amara shook her head.

"Speaking of which, on a different matter, what are your intentions toward Heron?"

"My . . . what?" Emmi sat up and blinked.

"You no longer tend them, so you are free to pursue a closer relationship." Amara twiddled her thumbs.

"Surely that's no one's business but mine and Heron's whether I do or don't, and whether I want to or not." Emmi shifted to sitting, feet firm on the ground.

"Yes I'm sticking my nose where it doesn't belong, but I'm fond of Heron." Amara swung her legs over and took a similar posture. "I'm not certain either of you appreciate the complexities involved."

"I appreciate your interest, but—"

"Lie," Amara said with a cheery grin, but a steely glint in her dark eyes. "Has Heron ever talked to you about Kitiva? About how matters of love are arranged very differently there?"

Breathing shallow, Emmi swallowed hard, torn between insulting Amara and going, or staying and having her deepest wishes possibly unraveled and examined.

Amara waited. At length, Emmi gave a short nod. Heron and she had discussed the matter on occasion over the years.

"In Kitiva, women court, but men choose," Amara said.

"Heron might have mentioned that." Emmi shrugged.

"But did you consider what it means? Women express interests and court whom they wish, but the men choose whether or not to move forward, whether as a one-night affair up to a long-term relationship. These are the most basic rules, the bones on which every other understanding is built."

Emmi shrugged again, as a lump formed in her stomach.

"What is the first and most important rule of attraction at court?" Amara asked.

"Consent matters." The answer practically fell off Emmi's tongue.

"I wish we were that positive, but I fear we stress the negative first." Amara shook her head. "I distinctly remember the Terparchon's meeting with Heron when she invited them to join the court as a princess. She warned them not to abuse their power."

"They haven't."

"Nor will they, but think about the assumptions underlying these two approaches." Amara held up a finger on each hand. "Women court but men choose versus do not abuse power. These tie Heron's hands. Heron belongs to Codaros now and we hope to keep them, but they will never *not* belong to Kitiva too. If you decide enter into a relationship with Heron, you must accept that you will never fully understand each other."

"Does anyone?" Emmi swallowed too late to keep back the retort.

"A fair point." Amara nodded. "Still, it is best to make a clear assessment of the situation before deciding whether to forge ahead."

Emmi left nearly shaking at Amara's presumption, even if she was trying to protect Heron—from what, from Emmi?

Yet as Emmi descended the stairs far slower than she'd climbed, one hand on the railing for balance, she had to admit that even as Amara was wrong she was also right. She'd provided a likely explanation as to why Heron had made no moves toward courting Emmi for years. They were waiting for Emmi to indicate her interest. To court them, despite the power difference.

Even though Heron and Emmi were no longer tangled in the roles of tended and attendant, Heron still had more power and influence than Emmi.

They might never make the first move.

Yet what had happened the day before? Maybe they thought Emmi had shown interest. She'd touched them—such smooth, warm skin— and they'd kissed her hand immediately after.

The first time they'd ever touched her.

Emmi had said they could talk about things another time, after Susa called for her. Heron had agreed, but what had they thought she meant by speaking later?

She might still have to decide whether or not to make a move. Was Heron worth the risk? The prospect scared her to the point she stopped midstep, clung to the railing, and struggled for breath.

For clarity, for surety, for anything to help her decide whether or not to take the leap and court them.

$ 8 $

Heron missed Emmi again that morning, even though Fotis did everything as Emmi had. Rather, almost everything. The eleee barely spoke or made eye contact with Heron, so different from Emmi's cheery greetings and the measured way she listened to them or offered ideas.

Dressed in simple tunic, mantle, and sandals, with the only cords at their waist attesting to their rank and their memory keeper tucked under their tunic as usual, Heron strode into the dancing pavilions for what would likely be the last practice of all princesses and compeers together before the court split. Nearly two dozen people generated a fair amount of warmth, apart from the sun streaming through the windows casting angled shadows on the floor. The tang of sweat remained, nearly drowned under a half-dozen perfumes and scents as the others stretched on their own or in twos or threes.

Instead of music or someone counting the beats, the hum of gossip filled the room.

The Terparchon was absent, and her eldest daughter as well. Heron's fellow princess Melite confidently assured another princess that the two were off making the final decisions of which princesses and compeers would go where when the court split into three instead of the usual two.

Heron didn't particularly care which ruler they accompanied, as long as they and Emmi were assigned to the same section of court. The alternative meant three months without seeing her and discovering what might come to being between them.

Therefore, they passed the gossipers and searched for someplace to warm up far away from endless questions and idle chatter. On the far side of the room two people stretched, each with ample empty space around them.

Zora on the right, in pale blue apart from the gold-on-gold cords at her waist, and her brother Todor on the left, in gray but wearing the same colored cords.

Heron angled over to take a spot near Zora and begin stretching. Arms, midsection, legs. One calf complained, threatening a knot. They paused and massaged the muscles. The ache eased bit by bit.

Zora sat on the floor, legs wide and leaning forward until her nose touched the painted wood. She glanced their way, expression doing a quick flip from sorrow to agony to joy, or it appeared. They rarely understood her mood swings, despite being paired with her for dancing on a regular basis, but she was there when they needed her support in the Dance. In the end, that was what mattered.

"Are they talking about anything else?" Zora frowned.

Easy enough to guess what she meant. "No, not that I heard."

"Poor Todor." Zora shook her head as she pulled her legs together and wrapped her hands around her ankles. "He was never going to be heir, but now he has to hear everyone talking about it."

"Never?" Heron asked, dropping to the floor to do similar stretches. "He and Ylena made a good pair."

"I thought you of all people would know." Zora stopped stretching and shifted backward to lean against the wall. "He's a son, and the Terparchon always descends through the daughter line."

Heron blinked and missed a stretch, nearly poking themselves in the eye with a toe. Passing things along strict mother-daughter lines was not a practice they'd heard embraced often in Codaros. But if only daughters could inherit from the Terparchon, that still left Zora. "Did you want to . . ." They flushed and broke off, having gotten sucked into gossip after all.

"No. Never. Yes. Only on alternate full moon dreams." Zora's words tumbled over each other, as though different parts all fought to answer first. She scowled, then shook her head and gave a triumphant smile. "I can't. I'm not a princess."

"Neither is Nefeli." Heron felt bound to point that out.

"Ah, but she's a born compeer so she has magic in her bones." Zora rose, dusting off her tunic. "It's not the same, but it's close enough. And Nefeli's in love with a suitable princess, and partners her regularly. You're the princess I've partnered the most. Would you want to be Terparchon?"

"Never." Heron shuddered. The thought had never crossed their mind until then, and they let it go without a smidgeon of regret.

"Exactly," Zora said. "Mother made the right choice, the only choice."

Heron hadn't ever been partnered with a born compeer during a Dance, only with taught compeers such as Zora. Even so, they'd noticed that born compeers brought something extra, they always knew where to go and what to do to ensure their partners made the most of Dancing. Zora was fast on her feet and always ready to offer Heron support, but she guessed things wrong sometimes and headed left instead of right, or tried to help Heron leap instead of sink low.

But they had no argument with their partner.

If they could, they'd offer her a shield against the whispers and sidelong looks cast her way.

Before the gossip could reach a fever pitch, Amara strode into the chamber clapping her hands. "You've all been exercising your tongues enough. Let's get the rest of your bodies to work."

Within moments, she had them working through an intense sequence of moves and dances, with no time or energy to so much as think about gossip.

Afterward, Heron soaked as long as they could, alternating between the baths and steam room, until their aches eased. Clothed as simply as before, in a green-and-white striped mantle over a white tunic, they headed off in search of food.

Only to discover their feet failed to take them to their rooms or to one of the reception areas where they might find food.

Instead, they wound up at the summer palace library. Much smaller than the library at the winter palace, it occupied a rectangular building accessed through a lovely plaza complete with a tinkling fountain at the center.

Heron stopped right in front of the building, gazing up at the archway set in the center of silvery stones. Step by step, they moved forward through the doors into the antechamber. Water trickled from the top of an immense pink spiral shell at the center, down into the catch bowl below. Mugs hung from the near wall. Heron freed the top —a pretty thing glazed in deep blue—and filled it from the fountain. Drank deep, then put the mug aside in a basket partly hidden in a far corner.

Baskets of luminescent mosses offered soft light to fill the chamber, which lacked windows. Small alcoves lined one side of the chamber. Beyond the fountain sat the double doors to the library, with grates set in them so the librarians could bar themselves within and check to see who came to visit before deciding whether or not to admit them.

As far as Heron knew, no one ever used the little grates. The librarians left the doors unlocked during public hours. Indeed, the righthand swung open at the lightest touch.

Heron had sworn they wouldn't get war dances information for Kitiva and told Stork as much.

Their feet evidently had a different idea. Blame their feet. Blame their head.

Blame the one time they carried messages through a war zone.

Not in Codaros, which had been peaceful for nearly a decade although the previous Terparchon had doubled the land after conquering several cities and their surrounding territories.

Rather, about the same time rulership had turned over in Codaros, Heron had been sent up into the mountains north of Kitiva, where two cities, two of Kitiva's valued trading partners, had descended into battle to determine control of a river that passed between them.

The cities started fighting in summer, kept on through autumn and into winter.

Heron still remembered walking across a battlefield that had frozen. Blood stained the ice. Everywhere they looked, they found red mixed with spots of black and green, guts and gore. Despite the care they took in picking their way across the field, they'd tripped over a corpse and landed near another trapped under frozen snow with a hand upraised seeking release.

Heron was born Kitivan, raised Kitivan. No matter how long they lived in Codaros, that wouldn't—couldn't—change.

Kitivans didn't want war.

Heron didn't want war. Hoped Codaros never attacked Kitiva or the other way around. What if they did? The Terparchon ruled with a light hand, allowing the cities and territories her mother had conquered to continue mostly as they had with certain adjustments: use of the same weights and measures as the rest of the land, the same overarching laws with some allowance for local practices, and careful accounting of the movement of people and possessions.

She'd allowed Heron to become a princess and maintain connection to their homeland, asking only that they abide by the laws and general customs of Codaros. Their place as a princess, and the Terparchon's need for princesses, had protected them to some extent—but if Codaros and Kitiva battled?

For a moment they considered turning around and going off in search of food, but instead they marched straight through the doors into the library proper.

They always forgot how light and airy it was, with tall, arched windows set in the thick walls and angled so as to provide natural illumination with as little direct sunlight as possible. A series of wooden shelves held scrolls and volumes enough to keep any reader busy for months if not years.

A librarian glided over to inquire how they might help. A familiar figure, Rhoda who stood a head shorter than Heron. Their ear-length dark hair boasted a few more gray strands than the last time Heron had spoken with them. Their long face, angled cheeks ruddy as though wind-chapped, lit with a broad smile. Uncaring of fashion, they wore two layered tunics in brown and soft slippers.

"I'm not sure." Heron had often visited the palace libraries in search of more information about Codaros, princesses, and dancing. They'd known about princesses and princess magic before turning into one to their surprise, but Kitiva rarely had more than one princess at a time. Heron remembered rumors about the old Kitivan princess of their youth jealously guarding their place and resenting even their chosen apprentice.

This interest had enabled them to ask questions about the type of dances that might make a difference for Kitiva, albeit only thanks to the Terparchon's expressed indulgence.

"Anything new about unusual dances?"

"We have the book of old tales that Danissa used for her ritual if you'd like to see it."

"Of course." Heron hadn't been present to see the other princess Dance her poisoned father back to health, but they'd heard the tale a dozen times over and at least thrice from people who had seen it firsthand.

What they wanted most was to find the compendium of dances supposedly assembled three rulers earlier, offering a full account and description of every type of dance ever performed by the full twelve dancing princesses plus Terparchon. It belonged in the winter palace library, except when it vanished, which it did regularly. Despite an unmistakable red-and-gold binding edged with silver and gold cords, it had a tendency to appear and disappear without warning no matter how the librarians tried to protect it.

Heron had yet to even see it.

The collection of stories would have to suffice.

Rhoda led them to a table and set out an old volume with a worn spine. It opened readily to the story about a wandering princess from ages earlier. Heron settled onto a bench and paged through stories after stories, many about Dances requiring three, five, or seven princesses.

Three Danced fruit trees from seed to maturity to feed a hungry village.

In a different tale, seven convinced a flood to change its course and spare another town. The citizens were so delighted they memorialized the deed in a mural on a wall.

A mural, a painting.

Impossible to find, if it even existed, though Heron had passed through many towns in every part of the continent with painted walls showing one scene or another.

For that matter, the summer palace was full of mosaics showing previous Terparchons and Marchons conquering cities, combining territories, and developing a unified system of justice and trade. Perhaps they might offer insights into war dances.

Their feet led the way again as they meandered around the palace complex in overlapping circles without any particular destination in mind, merely to note what mosaics they could find of battles and wars.

At least two offered possibilities worth coming back to study—and were in places Heron might sit and stare without being underfoot or obvious.

First, they paused before a wall on the eastern side of the royal dwelling that bore a long mosaic with several images of a Terparchon whirling through an army. It wasn't the current or the previous, but otherwise Heron had no idea who had inspired the image. Surely the ruler hadn't single-handedly routed the opposing force, shown as blank faced-figures raising spears or lying dead on the ground.

A storm loomed overhead, dark clouds save for a bright sun behind the initial figure of the Terparchon. She appeared first standing stalwart with her head high and arms at her sides. The second image portrayed her leaping, arms rising high. In the third, she cast lightning bolts at the soldiers.

The current Terparchon never leapt when Dancing storms, but had deflected lightning on occasion with flicks of her hands.

In all, the image suggested Dances easing nature could also be turned to rouse it in defense—or to cause deliberate harm.

Two plazas to the north lay a large mosaic set in the earth wherein an army was surrounded by a ring of twelve princesses plus the Terparchon. Each was posed slightly differently. All of the tiles had a ruddy color as though the image were washed in blood. Some princesses had hands poised to throw, even as the other mosaic had shown. Others leapt and kicked. Two hunched their backs and blew flames or ice.

Heron couldn't look at it for long without seeing again the bloody field of ice, snow, and corpses. They staggered away. Feet—or whatever back-of-the-brain instinct had led them—gave up and instead they followed whatever struck them as holding the opposite of war.

Laughter.

Joy.

Accident or accidental purpose? They ended up near the children's palace. This time they approached from the east, at the far end of the waist-high wall surrounding the play area.

Two younglings giggled as they tussled over a swing.

Three playing closer to the building dug bucketfuls of earth as they built a mud palace bearing no resemblance to any building in the complex.

Heron leaned against the wall, propping their elbows on the flat stones atop. The sights and sounds of the children's pleasure in play helped ease away memories of blood.

Except mixed within the chuckles and cries to "look at me!" came a sniff. Then a second one, both very close at hand.

On the other side, down where the base of the wall met the earth, a figure in a dirt-stained yellow tunic huddled with their arms wrapped around their legs. The child had buried their face against their knees, but Heron recognized the soft, silky black strands and growing limbs.

One of the attendants near the children's palace watched. They met Heron's gaze.

Heron pointed at themselves, then Susa.

The attendant shrugged but didn't stop watching. No doubt they'd intervene if warranted.

Heron drew in a deep breath. "Hi Susa, what's wrong?"

"Oh." She looked up and sniffed, round tears trickling along her cheeks. "It's you."

"You know who I am?"

"One of mama's princesses." She laid her head back against her knees, although she'd turned her face to the side. One dark eye looked forward, then up, and back.

"Exactly, except I'm not your mother's princess anymore." Heron sighed. "She's taking care of a compeer now."

"Princess, compeer." Susa shrugged. "Uncle-aunt says there's not much difference, as all of you need people walking around behind picking up after you."

Not exactly how Heron viewed the situation, but true enough. Considering the matter seemed to slow the track of tears, so they said, "Your mother does that very well."

"She should cook instead, like uncle-aunt." Susa lashed out with a fist, the edge hitting the wall. With redoubled tears, she shook her hand and tucked it under her chin. "Then we could *stay here*."

Aha, the progress was the problem, the need to leave. "All your friends will go on progress too."

"Only half of them." Susa sniffed and scowled.

Surely all, but she probably only counted the half accompanying whichever section of court she and Emmi went with.

"And we'll have to walk and walk and walk." Her body arched with each word until she sprawled prone on the earth.

"You have a point." The first days of the progress rarely went well as people who'd gotten used to staying in place had to remember how to travel across distances. Heron rested their arms atop the wall again and peered down. "But you could ride in a wagon some of the time."

"Bouncy, bumpy, stinky." She seemed happy to go on in that vein.

"Yes." Heron nodded agreement. "But then you get to see all sorts of strange sights. Did you know there are bogs where if you step off the trail, you could get sucked in over your head?" Heron made a gulping noise and clutched at their neck.

In truth, they'd only gotten their foot stuck the one time they'd tried that. It was on their second long-distance trek for the Kitivan council, and they'd not yet learned to decipher which pieces of advice to follow and which to ignore. After standing still for an hour while their guide oiled their foot free, they believed locals offering warnings.

Susa remained flat on her back, but her gaze kept flicking toward Heron.

What other sights might intrigue a child?

"Have you seen the enormous falls down the river from the lake, near Erevestis? They're taller than the palace!" Higher than two palaces, for that matter. The river narrowed where the water poured down. When the wind blew in the wrong direction, the spray dampened everyone and everything venturing near, and day or night one could hear the steady roar—even feel it in the back of one's teeth. "And so noisy, you can't hear anyone right next to you unless they yell."

That got her head shifting a little.

"Up north, there are cliffs hung with icicles taller than me." Heron stretched their arms up high. "They hold an ice festival at the heart of winter, and people compete to carve them."

Susa still didn't speak, but the more Heron described wonders they'd seen in their journeys, the fewer tears slid down her cheeks and the brighter the glint of interest in her face. She even smiled a few moments before her mother arrived to pick her up.

Happy accident that Heron was still around, or had they unconsciously planned it? They weren't sure.

But even across the distance they caught the tension in Emmi's body as she noticed them. How she paused and sucked in a deep breath before going to the gate to call for Susa.

Susa gave Heron a farewell wave, albeit only a flicker of her fingers, as she raced along the wall and into her mother's embrace.

Lucky Susa.

Heron straightened. Their body protested the long minutes spent leaning down and peering at Susa. They rolled their shoulders and pressed fists against the muscles at the small of their back. Closed their eyes, the better to not see Emmi walking away.

Only to open them at the soft double footfalls drawing near.

Emmi and Susa followed the line of the wall and stopped at the corner, facing Heron across a narrow space. Susa clung to her mother's hand, jiggling up and down as though her feet refused to touch the earth for long. Emmi gazed at Heron with shadowed eyes.

"Apparently there are all manner of interesting places to see along the progress, and I've been cruel to Susa by not telling her about them or taking her to see them." Emmi rested a fist on one hip.

"I was just trying to distract . . . ah . . ." Heron ran fingers through their hair. Then the world stopped a beat as a smile filled Emmi's face with light and humor. "Perhaps you could come to dinner and tell us about them?"

"Say yes!" Susa lurched across and grabbed Heron's hand, practically dragging them closer.

Susa clearly wanted Heron to come, but there was room for doubt whether Emmi invited Heron for Susa's sake or her own or both.

Still, with a chance to spend time with the two of them—and be warmed by the love flowing between them—Heron couldn't say no.

❦　9　❦

Emmi had too much to do before leaving Yaras to think about Heron. She never paused in the midst of packing her and Susa's belongings to remember the hesitant expression on Heron's face when they settled on the floor opposite Susa for dinner and then enchanted the girl with stories of far-off places. Emmi never took extra care in folding Zora's dance tunics and mantles—under Zora's watchful eye—because they resembled Heron's in all but size. Of course Emmi walked a short straight route between work, the children's palace, and her and Susa's rooms without lingering near the princesses' hall or dancing pavilion in hope of seeing Heron.

And Emmi absolutely, positively, refused to let Aurel's scowls get to her, after Susa chattered to her uncle-aunt about Heron's stories.

Emmi hardly required Aurel's whispered advice to find herself some fun with anyone but Heron, delivered even as he came to wave Emmi and Susa off.

But when the progress began, Emmi *truly* spent little thought on Heron!

For all of the first day or so.

Walking around the palace, even with climbing uncounted flights of stairs, hardly resembled the careful, measured pace required to accompany the Marchon on progress through the southern lands. The progress organizers had goals for how far everyone had to move each day to keep on schedule and reach Tharis before the start of winter. The first days' goals were less than they'd walk by the end—but still tough.

Feet, legs, and hips hurt. Sandals developed new ways of rubbing against one's heel, creating sores that no amount of herbs, creams, or padding could prevent from twinging for days.

One had to re-learn the best way to roll in blankets so as to sleep on the ground. The Marchon and a few of his closest retainers and guards took rooms at inns or houses in villages, when available. Most of court, which most assuredly including Emmi and Susa, camped. They put up tents of varying sizes and degrees of protection against water when the Marchon lingered to meet with local dignitaries and slept under the stars when on the move.

All that and dust, too! Only the fortunate travelers in the vanguard of the progress escaped—and even they got coated when the wind blew the wrong way. The summer sun had baked the earth along the tracks connecting villages, towns, and cities to the point they cracked and crumbled. The grit got into everything: shoes, bedrolls, food.

Susa complained about everything, not least uncle-aunt having stayed—perhaps wisely—in Yaras—and how much the oxen smelled.

Emmi happily turned her daughter over every morning to the children's attendants who set up a mini children's palace around several of the ox-pulled wagons. She and other parents also took turns watching over the young crew—most, but not all, as grumpy and whiny as Susa. It was only fair to let the children's attendants escape now and then.

Yet for all of the miseries of travel, the progress offered odd pleasures too. The oddest but most welcome, to Emmi, was how the lines in the court shifted. People who normally wouldn't have noticed or spoken with Emmi, or Susa, smiled and exchanged pleasantries. Clerks, cooks, and courtiers mingled and ate meals together, topping each other's tales of misery with as much laughter as tears.

All of the princesses and compeers spent at least one day trudging alongside Emmi.

Zora taught Susa bad jokes—mostly beginning with "knock,

knock,"—that the child insisted on repeating to Emmi until she wanted to plug her ears.

Excited at the prospect of going home for however short a visit, Gisela told Emmi all about the village she'd grown up in—completely forgetting that Emmi had visited it when accompanying the expedition that fetched Gisela to become a princess. Gisela's lover, the born compeer Stevan, stopped by to talk to Susa several times, regularly entertaining her by telling the child where her friends were and what they were doing.

Even Amara fell into step with Emmi and Susa on occasion. On a rare rainy day, Amara and Emmi helped each other wring waterlogged fabric and knock clods of heavy mud from their sandals.

Heron was the greatest help. They never spent a whole day with Emmi or Susa, but stopped by each day once or twice for a little while. Whether or not Susa's steps lagged before Heron showed up, after they shared tales of their adventures traveling around the continent, Susa always picked up her pace and forged forward determined to match them someday.

Perhaps Susa couldn't tell when Heron paused in the middle of any story and skipped something, but Emmi had learned to listen to Heron's silences. To suspect on occasion Heron had fled cities just ahead of a mob, or the ruler's minions. Or, worst of all, catch the fleeting twitch of their eyes holding back tears as they omitted something that had saddened them.

Susa wasn't the only one to invite Heron to stay with them for many an evening meal. So much easier to lean against them as she massaged Susa's feet and legs. Or be able to leave Susa listening to Heron's tales while Emmi juggled Zora's demands.

Though with each tale and meal, Susa developed a possessive air about Heron, similar to her attitude toward her uncle-aunt: sometimes presenting them to her friends as though sharing something precious, and other times trying to keep them away, to herself.

Then Susa started interrupting when Heron talked to Emmi. One night, she stamped and scowled, saying that Heron was *Susa's* friend.

"Mine too," Emmi said.

"Mine first." Another stamp, after which Susa refused to accept or admit that Emmi knew Heron before Susa.

Emmi appreciated that Heron did little to support Susa's attitudes, but grew concerned that they humored and indulged the child. They allowed her to steer them away from others, to demand two, then three tales in a row. Offered four, five, or six explanations when Susa complained about Heron going to walk or have meals with other travelers. Acquiesced to her demands that they stroke her hair as she fell asleep.

"You're not doing her any favors." Emmi drew Heron aside one night.

"I haven't had much to do with children." They shrugged, rubbing at their cheek and managing to miss the last spot of dust up by their ear.

"Then learn." Emmi crossed her arms, leaning against a scrubby tree. Susa lay snoring in her bedroll a few feet away, as did many other children and parents. A few lanterns glowed in the distance, where others remained up talking, and marking the lines where sentries watched. "I did. Others have. You can."

"What should I do?" they asked, head lowered.

She wondered if they might be hiding laughter in their eyes, but answered straight regardless. "Don't give into demands you wouldn't accept from anyone else. Set boundaries. If you say you have to leave, you have to. She must accept that."

"But she gets so sad."

"She does, she will, and sooner or later she'll have a tantrum." Emmi turned out her hands. She'd learned the hard way that she couldn't impose her desire for order on her daughter, who took partly after her disorderly father. "She'll be all right. You saw the to-do yesterday."

A child a year older than Susa had collapsed in the road after something had gone wrong. They'd yelled loud enough to be heard at either end of the progress. Screamed so hard Emmi's throat hurt in sympathy. Slammed fists against the dusty earth. Kicked and hit when two young attendants lifted them and tucked them in the back of a wagon pulled by a particularly patient pair of oxen.

One of the attendants swung onto the cart, sitting atop a pile of bedrolls, and stayed with them. Not touching, not speaking, but keeping company until the child dissolved into a sobbing mess, at which point the attendant offered comfort and a shoulder to cry on.

Heron shivered and gulped. "I'll try."

And they were as good as their word, which unfortunately increased the odds that Susa would have a meltdown soon. She hadn't had one yet, although most children did sooner or later, and the longer the wait the worse Emmi feared the outburst might be.

Nor was that the only unpleasant aspect of the progress.

Despite amusing Susa, Zora proved as much or more of a pain.

Actually tending to Zora wasn't much harder than serving anyone else. Zora adjusted quite well to sleeping on the ground in a bedroll, with no complaints about the hardness or chill, and no requests for Emmi to find a better spot next time that was flat instead of slanted or bumpy.

Likewise, Zora offered no complaints about Emmi's care for her clothing. She never pointed out wrinkles or stains and demanded they be cleaned. Neither did other princesses or compeers, but Emmi over-heard many courtiers whining as badly as the children.

No, the problems with Zora rested on two inescapable matters.

First, Zora was incredibly possessive of her things. She refused to divide her belongings into those needed ready at hand for the trek and things packed away in trunks and dug out only when the progress stopped in a city for a week or two. No matter that the trunks had stout locks and Zora kept the keys on her person, she insisted that two of her trunks be brought in rotation to her tent—when they stayed outside a village long enough to justify putting it up—or bedroll— when they were on the move—every night so that she could open it and go through to check that everything was where it was supposed to be.

Much as Emmi approved of order and everything in its place, there was such a thing as going too far.

She got the dubious honor of keeping records for Zora on the condition of everything in the trunks, noting down any damage to trinkets, scrolls, books, and her most elaborate clothes. The unpacking and packing Zora took care of personally, sometimes caressing one or another item with an odd glint in her eyes.

Emmi still hadn't figured out which of Zora's selves was which, or if each had their own name. The possessive Zora showed up whenever wrist deep her trunks. Zora's leading self sometimes let slip an apologetic grimace when asking for it, but didn't fight the possessive one over the matter.

Still, that wasn't quite the worst of things.

Which was the cat.

Homer had his own travel basket, which he detested. Zora could put the cat in with relatively little trouble, one or two scratches at most. Sometimes she asked Emmi to do so, and Homer did not like Emmi any more than she liked him. She counted herself lucky if she got away without scratches or oozing blood.

Zora took Homer on walks morning and night. While going through her trunks, Zora either put him in his basket or let him hang around her tent, lazing near but not too near.

The cat seemed to detest Zora's obsession with her trunks and belongings. He meowed and hissed, then turned his back and pouted when Zora didn't stop fussing over her belongings and come caress him.

Until the night he wandered off.

Emmi never forgot Amara's warning and kept a watch on the creature. Even when kneeling next to Zora and taking notes on the condition of Zora's belongings.

All the same, she missed the instant Homer vanished. He was there, then he wasn't.

The main Zora noticed before Emmi, pushing aside her possessive self and turning pale and shaking as she called for Homer.

He didn't return.

Emmi and Zora searched and called for the creature until the sky was almost full dark and the moon beginning to rise.

Then Zora's possessive self reappeared and locked the trunk. Told Emmi to stop fussing. "The cat will come back or it won't, and good riddance."

Trekking through the maze of sleepers to a nearby copse of trees,

Emmi found Susa leaning against Heron listening to a story . . . and stroking Homer.

He purred and rubbed against Susa's hand, but hissed when Emmi drew near.

Homer refused to allow Emmi to take him back to Zora, but allowed a sleepy Susa to carry him.

Susa stared up at Zora. Her lower lip trembled as she held Homer out.

The cat hissed—at Zora. Possessive Zora.

Whose eyes focused on the beast and the child holding him, lips pulling back in a snarl.

The compeer's body jerked. A moment later, main Zora or another self took over. Zora knelt in front of Susa and lifted the cat. A loud purr resounded as Homer rubbed its head against Zora's chest, leaving hairs behind that glittered silver in the burgeoning moonlight.

Heron laid a tentative hand on Emmi's shoulder, steadying her. They swept up a tired, teary Susa and carried her back to her bedroll. Before leaving, Heron leaned close to Emmi.

"Zora won't do anything to Susa, I'm certain. But perhaps we should keep Susa away from Homer."

"Or the cat away from her, but I'm not sure that will be possible." Emmi sighed, then managed a shaky smile. "If I haven't said it often enough, thank you."

"No need for that." Heron ducked their head, the movement making stubble along their chin cast long shadows. "It's been a pleasure."

"You've done so much." Emmi bit her lip, then stepped in close enough to bask in the warmth pouring off their body. "Amara reminded me about Kitivan customs, that women court and men choose. But you've been . . ."

"I'm not a man or a woman, no matter what Kitivans say." Heron brushed a tremulous finger along Emmi's cheek. "And it's not courting I've been doing, it's caring."

They slipped away without another word.

Emmi dropped onto her blanket and pulled the ends around her shoulders for warmth. Heron's words had made her tingle—and worry. She stroked her daughter's hair, smoothing away a stray cat hair.

Heron was caring, not courting—though Emmi hadn't asked them, or started courting them. The longer this went on, the harder any break would be when it came.

This wasn't like Emmi. She didn't invite messiness into her life. Too much came in on its own. She kept things clean and tidy. For years she'd balanced attraction and service in an orderly manner. Stood tall and strong when Susa needed a parent to lean on. Withstood her sibling's meddling.

Only to become a sapling in the wind, bending this way and that.

Much as Emmi appreciated Heron's strength and assistance, it wasn't fair to either of them to rely on them while so much remained unsettled.

Better to make a decision—to court or not—and stick to it. Her hands shook and belly roiled. Vague memories from months, years, back flashed through her mind: Heron talking about Kitivan courting customs. However had they gotten onto the subject? Surely Heron had been approached by a Codaran courtier interested in them, asked for help.

Maybe Amara could help, for Emmi would prefer not to ask Heron about it.

Or talk to them about the matter.

Not *yet*.

✣   10   ✣

When in doubt, Heron focused on the requirements of the day. Unfortunately, this morning that had resulted in their current location: in the midst of wagons loaded high with trunks and wicker baskets and bundles wrapped in lengths of hardy cloth. Their bare feet rested on warm packed earth, but fortunately the oxen grazed placidly in a nearby field and the few signs of their former presence among the wagons had been raked away or covered in straw.

Their body was limber from stretches, and a hint of starmeg from breakfast lingered on their lips. A loose, plain tunic flapped around their ankles, the reason for their presence in the wagons.

Thuds and grunts and hard-to-understand words marked the scattered presence of teamsters checking the conditions of the wagons. Two lounged against the closest wagon, tunics already unfastened at one shoulder and a faint sheen of sweat on their chests, as Fotis scrambled about it trying to locate Heron's missing trunk.

One of the teamsters muttered about how Fotis should've marked it better, because the teamsters knew to put the princesses and compeers' dance stuff where it was easily accessible and it wasn't their fault this had gone missing.

The other hummed a tune. The more distant teamsters picked it up and started humming or singing along, no two in the same key.

Heron closed their eyes and for a few moments imagined themselves home during a festival.

Then a loud crash made them jerk. A trunk fell off, lock breaking and tunics and mantles spilling out onto the ground.

Heron's, of course.

Fotis broke into a mix of apologies—to Heron—and semi-coherent scolding for the teamsters.

"Take care of the rest." Heron scooped up a suitable set of clothing for dancing—a lightweight pale gray tunic and deep red mantle embroidered in vines of silver and gold. "I'll go get myself ready."

"But—" Fotis bit their lip, concern clear on their face.

"I've done it before. It'll be fine. You just deal with this mess. One thing at a time." With scarce a look back, Heron escaped. Winding their way through the maze of wagons and tents to theirs went fast enough.

Likewise they made short work of dressing despite having to kneel on their bedroll. The tent still smelled of wax from waterproofing. Thick branches supported the sides, but even someone short would have to stoop at the center. Perhaps the lines of their mantle weren't as crisp as desirable across their back, but who would remember? Heron couldn't see, so they didn't care.

They missed Emmi's efficiency. Fotis would surely become similarly organized in time—Heron had their own memories of stumbling in their early years as a messenger and, more recently, their first year as a princess. Heron merely had to wait through the growing pains—and remember that this was a small price to pay for the possibility of growing something more with Emmi.

"Heron."

They emerged as Susa called in the distance.

Heron's was one of several similar tents forming a circle, each of plain, waxed cloth and differentiated by their trim. None were large, for hey held two, perhaps three at best, but the area was silent. The other princesses and compeers had gone on ahead. Damp cloth flapped in the breeze, hanging from rope lines and draped across the tops of tents, making the usual varied colors twice as mixed and bright. The sun beating down roused a light haze of sweat on their brow, but the wind whisked it away.

They bent to fasten the ties of their sandals, gold ribbons wrapping around their calves and fastened at the knee, memory keeper swinging against the inside of their robe. Then they stood tall and waved at Susa, searching the forest of tents for signs of Emmi and finding none.

Swallowing a sigh, they tried to hide any signs of disappointment as Susa trotted over followed by a youngling perhaps twice her age. Both were dressed in simple beige tunics and no mantles, plain ropes wrapped two or three times around their waists. Susa's hair was pulled back into a single fall down her back. The older had darker skin of warm brown, a round face with a snub nose rather than narrow, and dark hair cut to shoulder-length, but both were all legs and arms and might be distant relations.

"There you are!" Susa ran toward them, stopping short and pressing clasped hands against their chest. "Everyone's going, but want I to go with you. May I? Please please please?"

"Go where?" Heron blinked, glancing around but seeing no children other than Susa.

"The progress children have been invited to visit Foleilion and meet the children who live here, and watch the dancing." The older had a light, breathy voice. On second glance, perhaps they were more than twice Susa's age, and one of the children's-palace attendants accompanying the progress. "Susa asked if she might come with you, if you're willing."

"They are." Susa stamped, lips turning down at the corners. "You can go with everyone else, Edrena." Then, with less assurance, Susa bit her lip and turned to Heron. "You will, won't you?"

"All right." It would be nicer to have company, though Heron couldn't help wishing Emmi was with Susa.

The child leapt forward, a blazing smile stretching their face.

"Hand or rope?" Edrena coughed, gaze focused on Susa.

Susa stopped less than an arm's length from Heron. Her chest rose and fell as she heaved a tremendous sigh, eyes rolling. "You want hands, right?"

"I don't understand." Heron glanced beyond her at her attendant.

"Susa, you want to explain?" Edrena smiled at Heron over Susa's head, turning hands out to either side.

"We gotta stick together, so nobody gets lost, but not everybody wants to be touched, and we're not supposed to guess or think we know just cause they didn't mind holding hands some other time. We gotta ask." Susa gave another sigh. "So, do you want hands or rope?" She patted the rope at her waist.

"Hands would be fine." Heron hadn't thought how children in Codaros learned not to touch, or to take care, when Kitivan younglings grabbed with little censure. Despite a mote of curiosity as to how Susa would handle the rope—unwrap her belt and hold one end with Heron on the other?—Heron stretched out their hand.

One far smaller, not even half their size, slipped into it. Soft and warm as Emmi's, but without Emmi's muscles and callouses. A precious trust.

"I'll watch over her." They met Edrena's gaze and nodded.

"Good enough." Edrena turned to Susa. "And Susa, once you get to the village, you'll go play with the other children, right?"

"No." She shook her head, long tail of hair flying and brushing Heron's arm. Her fingers clutched tighter. "I'll stay with Heron."

Heron bent down to roughly Susa's level. "Why not play with the others? You'd be bored staying with me. I have"—they searched for the right words—"dull things to do before dancing."

"I wanna stay with you!" Susa sniffed.

The glint of moisture in her eyes hit Heron hard, but Emmi had warned them not to give into Susa on everything. They needed to prove faith and trust to parent as well as child.

Or maybe they could find a compromise.

"How about if you walk back with me after?" Heron glanced at Edrena. "If it's all right?"

"As long as you don't stay there too late, it should be fine." Edrena made a face. "I'm only temporary help, so I can't say anything for certain, but I don't think it should be a problem."

The result was a sulky Susa clinging to Heron as they wound over to the edge of the tents to meet the other princesses and compeers.

From there, Heron hoped someone knew the right path and turns to take to reach the village. This wasn't anywhere Heron had visited on previous progresses.

Susa refused to let go of Heron's hand even when Zora joined them.

The royal compeer had chosen similar colors to Heron, dark red mantle over a white tunic. Her arms cradled her cat, who purred when she bent and let Susa stroke it.

Emmi followed behind, raising an eyebrow at Susa, who clung all the tighter to Heron and leaned against them.

"Susa was given permission to walk to the village with me, though she's supposed to play with the children while there," Heron said.

"You promise?" Emmi turned a stern look at Susa.

"Yes." Susa's chin jutted out and she didn't look at her mother, busy petting the cat.

"Ready to head in?" Amara clapped her hands from the edge of the clearing, as other princesses and compeers trickled in to form a small knot.

Susa pouted as Zora handed the cat over to Emmi, with strict instructions to put him in the basket in the tent. Neither Emmi nor the cat was pleased as Emmi carried it off, with backward glances at Heron and Susa.

"Shall we?" Zora asked Heron, winking at Susa.

Zora on one side and Susa the other, Heron fell in behind Amara. A good three hands' width of space separated them from Zora, while Susa kept close. The child panted, keeping up a good pace, but showed no signs of faltering.

Amara had glanced at her and given a small smile, and set a pace the child could maintain.

Most of the progress had tented in fields left fallow or recently harvested. The rutted path leading to the village passed turnoffs to other fields visible through the trees, at least one with grain still ripening.

The Marchon was missing, but he'd spent the night in the village. It was too small to hold many more than him and a few others, including Gisela and her compeer, Stevan. Rumor said they'd slept on the floor of the village's council chamber, in conditions hardly better than the tents.

"Why ever did we stop here for longer than it takes to wave? It's nothing more than a speck on the map." Zora's nose wrinkled, and she quickened her steps to walk with Amara rather than Heron and Susa.

"This is where Gisela comes from." Amara's voice carried along the length of the procession. "We're here to visit and Dance in thanks for her joining us."

"And what are we to Dance, fertility?" Zora asked.

"No, stability." Amara paused, turning to stare at Zora. Heron and Susa stopped, and the rest of the princesses and compeers in a ragged group behind them. "These people, the Escalli, were driven off their homeland several generations ago by earthquakes that changed the shape of the river. They were given these lands, but have suffered occasional quakes here, too, over the years, so today we'll ease and firm the earth. It should not take long, and is an acceptable return for their having yielded Gisela to join us."

"But there's no underground chamber, and only half of us." The protest from behind could have been Teris or Iduma, princesses with similar voices and who'd both started dancing with the court in the past year, although in all other respects they differed.

"We have the hills and woods around us. We'll have less power, but make do." Amara gave a firm nod and started up again with Zora at her side.

"What's it all mean?" Susa asked in a whisper.

Her questions about what princesses and what kind of dancing they did kept Heron busy until they reached the edge of the village.

Buildings of brick and wood with thatched roofs formed a series of incomplete circles. In the distance, smoke rose from chimneys on the far side, and smells of roasting vegetables hung in the air. The earth was mostly well-packed, save for dips here and there that retained water from a recent rainfall.

The escorts who'd met them—a trio of elders all white-haired and dressed in loose green robes—offered simple descriptions of the different parts of the village. Here were the sheds and working areas where skilled weavers spun and wove cloths that brought distant traders to stop and bargain. The far side of the village was mostly dwellings. Regularly scrubbed privies were carefully situated among them with an eye toward balancing bodily needs and health interests.

As the princesses and compeers followed a slightly twisty route between edifices, they passed an oval area filled with children and ringed with adults watching them. It was easy to distinguish between locals and visitors. To Heron's eyes the Escalli resembled most of the southern peoples of Codaros, with deep tan skin, black hair, and triangular chins. Their clothes, however, were much simpler and boasted little decoration. Evidently any fancy fabrics they wove were mostly for trade.

The difference between the children was even clearer. Those who came from the progress wore tunics belted with rope, much like Susa. The local children ran around with only a simple length of cloth wrapped around their genitals.

Susa turned up her nose when Heron paused and urged her to join the others. It took Edrena and an older attendant from the progress coming over to half-drag Susa off with them before she left.

She cast reproachful glances at Heron as they turned to follow the other princesses and made the mistake of looking back.

Heron's skin was chilled without Susa's fingers tucked in their grasp. They buried their hand in their robes, a handful of cloth a poor substitute.

A chuckle from nearby made Heron start.

"Children do know how to pull on heartstrings." A stranger pushed away from the side of a building and walked over to Heron. Local, given the slow, crisp accent delivered in a mellow, mid-range voice—and plain green tunic which, although belted with length of twined ribbon, had a heavier, rougher look than the soft folds falling around Heron.

Ample gray streaked the other's short, dark hair and speckled the thin beard lining their cheeks and chin. Heavier fabric didn't conceal their high, firm breasts or the way their body curved in at the waist.

Heron had met many eleee over the years since they first ventured out of Kitiva. The first one they'd stared at, and by the third they'd begun to sidle over and whisper questions. By the seventh, they'd started to dare consider the term as including themself.

Yet old habits died hard. In all their travels, they'd never completely lost the tendency to look over people and tot up signs that, in Kitiva, would mark them as male or female. They'd never managed to *not* consider someone as an eleee without also acknowledging—if only to themself—that in Kitiva the person would be considered a man or a woman.

Until this moment. Eleee or not, Heron wasn't sure any Kitivan would be able to guess them male or female at sight.

For that matter, the other's age was also impossible to estimate. Gray streaks paired with youthful skin, including several pimples among the beard hairs, and a degree of vitality despite gnarled fingers.

All of which was none of Heron's business, so they blinked and managed to respond to the stranger's words. "Susa certainly knows how to pull my strings."

"Your first?" The stranger asked.

"Not mine, but the daughter of a"—Heron settled on a safe, neutral term—"friend."

"Then you're still learning?"

"Oh, yes."

Children's screams and yells echoed, making talking difficult. Checking ahead to ensure that Heron had not lost sight of the others —they had, but caught sight of Gisela, dressed to dance, emerging from a building and waving at them. Or at the stranger, for when Heron headed toward her, the other fell into step alongside. They matched Heron stride for stride, despite being shorter.

Gisela met them halfway. "Ah, you've found each other."

Heron glanced from her to the stranger and back.

"We have." The stranger nodded. "Though we've no idea who each other is."

Gisela laughed, then turned to Heron. "Allow me to introduce Alvi, who is the head of the village council."

"Soon to be former head." Relief shone on Alvi's face.

"Congratulations," Gisela said. "Alvi, this is Heron, a princess of Codaros and an eleee."

Heron held out a hand, a reflexive act that five years in Codaros hasn't completely eradicated on meeting a stranger, although half of the time they remembered to bow instead.

Alvi shrugged, then shook Heron's hand.

Both jerked as an intense bolt of energy shot through them.

An instant later, Alvi pulled in close. Their voice dropped although Gisela was only one close enough to hear. "Are you magical?"

"I'm a princess," Heron said.

"But are you a magical eleee?" Alvi asked.

Heron took a second glance over the odd mix that comprised Alvi's physical appearance. Impossible, and yet . . . "I didn't realize magical eleee really existed."

"Neither did I. I knew I wasn't the same as the few other eleee among us, but thought that was that, until a few weeks ago when these changed." Alvi grimaced and ducked their chin at their bosom. "Now, I need to learn more."

"I'd hoped you might know a magical eleee, even if you weren't one." Gisela shook her head.

"Maybe they're all hiding?" Heron shook their head. "I'm sorry I can't be of more help."

"I'd hide if I could." Alvi sighed. "Ah well, if none come here then I must go in search of them."

Someone shouted their name in the distance, and they headed off.

Gisela led Heron in the same direction. "I didn't realize. You will . . ." she laid a finger across her lips.

"Of course." Heron followed, finding relief in losing themself among the other princesses and compeers. Safety in numbers, or at least the ability to hide and think while drawing little notice. Magical eleee supposedly could change themselves and their bodies however they wished, and each could share that magic with one other person.

But Heron liked who they were, even though it had taken a long time to get to that point.

Dancing helped.

Villagers lined three sides of the square, the elders provided with seats at the front while others ranged behind. Children—locals mixed with those from the progress—knelt or sprawled in front. Many others from the progress had also come to the village, but took places farther back behind the locals.

Of all things, cats joined them as well. Smaller cats watched from atop human shoulders or cradled in human arms, while others sat on roofs or mingled with the children.

The Marchon and his chief aides mingled with the very oldest Escalli along the fourth side. Alvi appeared the youngest of them, nodding at Heron when their gazes met briefly.

But everything about Heron's surroundings faded when the time came to dance. All that mattered was the firm packed earth underfoot, the urge to move coursing through their body, and their fellow Dancers. Flute players wove an intricate melody, but more important was the incessant beat from two drums.

Amara partnered with the Marchon, leading the Dance. They traced a variant of an old court dance across the open space. Zora helped Heron align to the music and the earth. Sandaled feet slapping in time with the drums, Heron traced out regular patterns—squares and rectangles and the occasional oval.

At the start, the earth beneath held a ripple of restless movement. With each pass around the square, it eased. Quieted. Settled into place.

Minor magic compared to the great spells worked in chambers deep in the earth, but important all the same. Likewise, the Dance left Heron exhausted but at peace.

This was the first part of Codaros they'd come to love. They had so many more reasons to stay now, but this still ranked first and foremost. They Danced for Codaros because Dancing made things better, and always left them feeling better.

Not least this time, because they'd caught a glimpse of Emmi among the watchers. The villagers might not understand what the princesses had done for them. Emmi surely wouldn't.

But she'd seen them Dancing for the village—and for her.

Emmi's arms itched from Homer's scratches. The lines had dulled to a pink nearly invisible against her skin, but she could trace every line the cat had left with ease. Lotion helped, though sadly the one that worked the best so far included sonnewood as a prime ingredient. The scent clung to her, day in and day out, reminding her of her new duties—and the dratted cat—whether or not she wanted it.

Dressed in her usual plain tunic with an added mantle against the sudden morning chill, Emmi walked Susa through a stand of woods to the open field designated for the children's use. This was the second stop since Emmi had seen Heron Dance in Foleilion—and the longest so far, near five days just outside a large city—but the basic lines of camp rarely changed much. The administrators in charge of laying out the camps imposed the same layout on every site, adapting the bare minimum to the local landscape.

Distant birds called overhead as Susa yawned and dragged her feet. The girl knew the way on her own, but Emmi preferred to keep her company. Soon enough Susa would bound off and grow away.

"It's early." Susa's whine grated. Maybe Emmi wouldn't mind so much.

"Untrue." It was about the usual time, for the sun shone at a slanted angle that made all shadows twice their usual length.

Emmi twitched, scratches itching but everywhere else also aflame with nervous energy. For once she would not head next to fetch Zora's water. Emmi had traded tasks with Fotis and other attendants to make time—finally—for an overdue task.

Despite Susa's yawns, as soon as they emerged from the line of trees surrounding, the girl ran off to play with friends on a board precariously rocking atop a large boulder.

Emmi waited between the shadows of two trees, enjoying the warm sun on her shoulders.

Lysia, one of the older attendants minding the field, came over within a few minutes. The elder had a respectable wreath of white hair braided around her head, echoed in the pale gray trim on her blue mantle and the faint gray tinge to her beige skin. "We have her for all day?"

"Oh, yes. Since we're moving tomorrow, there's so much to be done." Emmi snapped her jaw shut, to keep from babbling more.

"Don't I know it. And turning north, this time. Soon we'll think this weather hot." Lysia waved at the distant sun.

"Do you need me to take her back early? So she's not underfoot." The attendants, after all, had to pack up the children's toys as well as their own belongings.

"They're never underfoot." Lysia nodded at the half-empty wagon sitting at an angle on the far side of the field. "With all these helping hands, we find ways to put them to work. As it happens, I'll be bringing Lorenza and Riki back over to your side of the camp at the end of the day. I could bring Susa as well, if you'd like."

"Are you sure?" Emmi's side of camp, but she recognized the names as the children of the Marchon's primary guards. Their tent lay several lengths away from Emmi's, but it was a kind offer. "You'll already have spent the whole day with them."

"If I didn't love children, I'd be in the wrong place of work." Lysia shook her head and laughed. "I'm tenting near you, anyway."

Emmi left the field with mixed feelings. Relief, for one less duty warred with unease at the prospect of her next stop. Gauging the passage of time with glances at the sky, she paused in the kitchen area long enough to drink a tall glass of spiced water. It washed down the last taste of her breakfast, but her stomach roiled all the same.

Better not to keep procrastinating.

Amara's tent sat three over from Zora and five from Heron, but Emmi refused to glance at either. She nearly tripped over her feet as she stumbled to a stop near the cloth covering the door right as Amara pulled it aside and emerged.

The retired princess had wrapped her hair in a length of purple cloth, a hair darker than the mantle draped around her shoulders and spilling over her pale pink tunic. The colors heightened the strange lavender tinge to her skin, giving her an otherworldly air.

The glint in her eyes as she gave Emmi a thorough looking-over made Emmi wonder if she'd missed a rent in mending or had a loose thread hanging off her shoulder.

"Do you . . . Can you spare some time?" Emmi asked.

"Of course." Amara let the door cloth fall behind her. "Would you prefer to come into my tent or shall we walk a wall together?"

Given the closed door cloth, Emmi chose walking. Perhaps she'd have been better forcing her way into the small expanse, but even though Amara's tent was slightly larger than Emmi's it would no doubt grow stuffy with two grown women inside.

The same could not be said of the direction in which Amara led Emmi. She'd evidently meant walking walls quite literally—but not those around the town. Instead, they passed through the line of guards stationed at the edge of camp, crossed the main road into the town, and proceeded along a low stone wall that ran between roughly rectangular fields on the far side. Emmi didn't recognize what crop the town had recently harvested.

The ground was mostly solid, but uneven. Bits of roots and dead vegetation lay scattered, light brown against the rich, darker sod. Black birds with bright red heads congregated in large groups scratching at the ground. With a loud cry, they'd rise, fly about, and land near where they'd been before.

Emmi opened her mouth more than once to speak, but each time Amara glanced at her and touched her lips. The older princess didn't say anything until they'd reached the far end and turned to follow the wall east.

"Which matter brings you to me?" Amara asked.

Emmi shivered at the other woman's emphasis on *'which.'* Did Amara think Emmi would complain about Zora? The royal compeer wasn't easy to tend to, but Emmi had managed. She'd keep on doing so, as long as she didn't have to hold the cat too often. Swallowing hard, she said, "you seem to know a fair amount about Kitivan customs."

Amara glanced at Emmi, but her voice was light as she spoke. "I spent time there."

"Heron told me something about courting customs, but that was years ago and I wasn't listening properly then," Emmi said.

"And now you need to know."

"Yes."

"What have you decided?" Amara led the way as they took another turn. The city loomed in the distance, chimney pots and taller buildings rising above the walls. The birds hunting in the field took flight and made a large swirling motion before landing right where Amara and Emmi had passed. A few rested on the wall near them, watching with baleful eyes.

"I don't know what it is that I need to decide." Emmi watched the earth, the better to avoid tripping as much as to avoid reading whatever lurked on Amara's features. "They said there was something about exchanges and gifts, and the gifts were supposed to mean a lot, or cost a lot."

"Kitivans are, or were, a very formal people," Amara said. "They have rules and laws and customs to cover most aspects of life, not merely courting. Still, before starting courting they consider it important to have some idea of what you want the end result to be. You remember that women court?"

"And men choose."

"A woman need not know exactly what she wants the end to be, but should have decided at least what results she doesn't."

Emmi paused, then had to take quick steps to catch up when Amara failed to do so as well. "Results?"

"Courting leads to choice leads to contract. Do you want Heron to sire a child and have nothing further to do with you or offspring? To sire and be a presence? Sire and help raise?" Amara counted off possibilities on long fingers. "Or perhaps not to sire, but to be a presence or help raise."

Halting and dropping to sit on the fence, Emmi clapped hands over her ears. She couldn't block Amara's voice.

"Alternatively, perhaps no siring or raising, but being a companion in bed only, in which case one must also decide for a set time or unlimited? Then there's another option which is to seek a companion for bed and more—"

"Stop. Please." Emmi rocked atop the uneven stones, her knees up near the center of her chest and shoulders hunched.

Amara retraced her steps to stand opposite, hands hanging loose at her sides.

"Do they really decide that much beforehand?"

"Most do." Amara nodded. "Though one can renegotiate as needed."

"So many possibilities. How can one know?" Emmi rubbed her forehead.

"The first step is to decide what you don't want versus what you might be interested in." Amara crouched down, amusement clear on her face. "Breathe. Think it through. Surely there's something you don't want."

That was easier, but not enough. Emmi didn't want another child, or at least she had no desire to court Heron to sire one, though if one happened, that was another matter. Nor was she after Heron to help her raise Susa, much as she appreciated his assistance. Easy also to admit that she wanted more than merely to share a bed for a limited time or longer, though the thought of being with them, touching them, made her giddy.

The problem remained what she wanted. Talking, yes. Regular contact, yes. The right to spend time with them, yes. Touching. Claiming? Sharing?

"But if I don't know, then how do I pick the gifts?" She stood, shaky at first but quickly steadying as she and Amara fell back into step and drew closer to the camp.

"Don't worry about gifts at the start. They're not important until you know what you want to ask of Heron."

"But if I'm to court them . . ." Emmi shook her head. "Are there flowers to avoid because they say the wrong thing?" She'd been showered with gifts once. Bouquet after bouquet, sometimes stuck in jars or vases and other times live plants despite the giver knowing full well Emmi couldn't easily carry them with her on progress. Each bloom supposedly meant something, and the giver had been disappointed when Emmi failed to understand.

"Forget flowers and things like that, they're how many peoples in Codaros show interest and affection, but not in Kitiva." Amara waved as the circling birds veered a little too close. "The *process* of courting involves only things you cannot buy or hold, such as time, attention, touch, and being very clear that you are offering these and asking for them in return. That should run long enough for you to decide what you want."

Gifts that one couldn't buy or hold. That alone eased a little of Emmi's tension. She was paid well enough for her work to live and send some back to her family, but there was a decided difference between what she purchased and what Heron could afford.

"At the end, you will need only two physical gifts, and these should be carefully chosen but need not be expensive. One is to represent what you are asking from them and the other what you are offering in return, and both reflect what you have learned of Heron, and they of you."

Emmi trailed a beat behind Amara as the elder threaded through the guards and back into the maze of tents.

"It's so complicated." Emmi sighed. All that she'd heard repeated over and over in her mind, until she forced it down. She would start small, with time and attention, and hope Heron understood.

As they approached Amara's tent, Homer strutted out of Zora's and spotted them. With a leisurely air, the cat turned around and sat down with its back to Emmi. Grunts and soft thuds suggested the cat had been ousted from inside the tent as Zora rose. A pitcher of water sat next to the cloth entrance, a hint of steam rising above.

"Complicated, yes, but Kitivans consider courting in Codaros to be messy and unclear. Then again, we are speaking of a people for whom much is written in stone. Denizens of Kitiva believe people are born formed but untrained and the task of a city is to raise its people." Amara drew a complex symbol in the dust before her tent. "Have you ever seen this?"

Emmi stared for several moment. "Yes." Though she wasn't sure just where or when.

She glanced aside as Zora left her tent and stretched. The royal compeer hefted the pitcher, grinning at the cat then turning a smaller smile at Amara and Emmi.

"It represents Kitivan citizens' duty to their city in balance to the city's raising of its people." Amara obliterated the symbol with a pass of her foot. "In Kitiva, one belongs to the city first and family after."

"A narrow view." Zora's voice turned cold, all traces of the smile vanishing from her face. The cat watched her, pausing in the middle of washing his face. "One should belong to the country first, then city, then the rest. Cities alone can do too little."

"So you say, and such has often been the will of Codaros," Amara said. "To make of all cities one country."

"Exactly." Zora's lips drew back from her teeth. She shivered, and the cat roused to rub against her legs. She turned to Emmi with a smaller, sadder smile. "Be sure to bring something special for Homer's dinner tonight, will you? Fresh caught fish, if one can be gotten, or something like that." She bent to pet the cat, who glared at Emmi.

"Of course." Emmi nodded.

"Do you have enough to go on?" Amara asked.

"Yes." Emmi closed her mouth before 'for now' could escape.

"If the time comes that you require gifts, I am willing to advise," Amara said.

Emmi thanked her and escaped gladly into work. It wasn't her favorite kind, there was nothing to truly tidy or scrub and be able to let her mind go as she labored, but Zora kept Emmi busy enough that she didn't have time to dwell on Amara's advice.

Until Emmi's work helping Zora pack and repack her belongings ended early so that Zora could head into the city to have dinner with her father and local dignitaries.

Emmi's shoulders and back ached as she headed back to her tent to ensure she and Susa were ready to leave in the morning. She checked behind several times to make sure the cat didn't follow. Its tail had lashed when she left, as it licked up the chopped fish she'd obtained, but she wasn't sure it would remain behind until halfway to her tent.

Susa hadn't returned yet, but Heron was there. Even seated, Heron was nearly as tall as Emmi's tent, for she and Susa had just enough space to lie down together. Fotis evidently took decent care of Heron, or their clothing, for Heron wore a soft green mantle over a lighter green tunic, and there was a neatly mended seam along the hem that Emmi hadn't sewn.

Small covered dishes sat on a tray perched on the flat top of Emmi and Susa's trunk. A hint of pepper in the air suggested they'd brought finger foods that could keep, along with a pitcher of water, which meant Emmi didn't have to go fetch dinner along with everything else.

"And you still say this is caring not courting?" Emmi dropped to her knees opposite them, feeling every aching muscle and each drop of perspiration on her brow or soaked into her wrinkled, stained tunic.

"It's a little thing." Heron shrugged. "I'm not needed for the farewell banquet in the city, when so many others want to go. So I thought I'd come here with simple foods that don't ask too much of the cooks."

"Yet here you are making my life easier through you paying time instead of me. Isn't that the kind of thing the person courting does?" Emmi shook her head, reaching for the covers on the dishes. The first, second, and third all proved to be dishes she or Susa favored. "Amara said—"

"Amara?" Heron sat straight, eyes wide.

Emmi ducked her head, feeling her cheeks heat. "I couldn't remember all you'd said about Kitivan customs, so I asked her."

Heron knocked the top off the dish with sliced peppers and nabbed one, crunching on it as they restored the top. Swallowing, they gazed across the tray at Emmi. "Do you mind telling me what she said?"

"That I have to decide what I want, or at least what I don't want." Emmi picked up a slice for herself, cradling the soft flesh in her hands.

"Siring, raising, sharing a bed, companionship, and how long, and . . . and . . . that Kitivans are very formal and have to decide everything in advance."

"She's not wrong, but we're not quite so . . ." Heron shook their head, lines furrowing their brow.

"Is she wrong about saying the most important thing is for me to know what I want?" Emmi sighed and set the pepper back in the dish, folding her hands in her lap. "Because I don't."

"Give me a moment?" Heron set their hands against the ground, needing the solid feel of the hard-packed earth beneath them. The world seemed to swirl around them, and the air turn thick and hard to breathe.

Nothing had changed—they still sat next to Emmi's tent, with her kneeling across from them. Dirt clung to the hem of her tunic, and her mantle hung limp around her shoulders with threads loose and the hem starting to unravel. Dust streaked her hair, interrupted where she'd run her fingers through the short strands.

Adorable, even more so when Heron considered what she'd admitted: that she'd asked Amara about Kitivan courting customs—and that she didn't know what she wanted from *Heron*.

Emmi looked relieved that Heron was taking time to think things through. She turned into her usual whirl of motion, retrieving clothes from the tent and sorting them, then folding them into neat piles ready to fill the trunk. In between folds, she sipped water and snuck slices of pepper dipped in yogurt.

All the while also regularly glancing sideways at Heron.

That she wanted to know meant a lot, no matter that she hadn't decided *what* she wanted from them.

Fair enough, because Heron wasn't sure exactly what they wanted, or what they could offer with their future unsettled. As their uncle had reminded them, they might not Dance for much longer. Still, they were certain and unshakable about one thing, now that the prospect opened up.

"I understand that you haven't figured out what you want, but"— Heron dragged in a whistling breath— "do you want to figure out what you might want? With me?"

Emmi blinked. "Do I what?"

"Do you want to start the courting process with me?"

"Ye-es." She dropped the mantle she'd started folding atop a pile of neat, squared cloths. One end hung down onto the ground, the rest in a messy heap. That she didn't immediately straighten it spoke to her nervousness.

"We're in Codaros," they said. "Kitivan customs don't apply here."

"But Codaros doesn't really have any customs, or maybe too many?" Emmi rubbed her hands. "Basic rules are not to abuse power and consent matters, but outside of that . . . it's very easy to start something and end up somewhere quite different wondering how everything got so messy."

Emmi's mouth had a bitter twist.

"Happens everywhere," Heron said, with their own hint of bitterness audible even to their ears.

"Even in Kitiva?"

"One of the kindest things one can do is to make clear up front what one doesn't want." Without bidding, a two-decade-old memory reverberated within Heron: a biting voice expressed surprise that Heron hadn't understand this was only a few nights of pleasure rather than the start of something more.

"Did that happen to you?" Emmi asked. "Someone not telling you?"

"More than once, but never the same way twice," Heron said. "I learn."

"I'm sorry you had to go through that."

"And I'm sorry for your mess."

"You guessed?" Emmi clapped her hands against her cheeks, then shrugged. "It probably wasn't hard."

"Will you give me the gift of telling me about it?" Heron shifted their seat, rubbing legs to head off pins-and-needles pain.

"Gift?"

"It's one of the things that can be shared during a courtship." Heron shrugged. "Past joys or sorrows, but only if you wish."

"A gift of sharing, that's a strange way of looking at things." Emmi shook her head. Her hands trembled as she topped up her mug with water, pitcher rim hitting the clay mug more than once.

Heron licked their lips rather than say that Codaros customs seemed as strange to them despite spending years learning them.

Perhaps Emmi caught the thought, for an exasperated huff escaped her, but she merely shifted her seat to stay opposite him. "The messiness, it was with Susa's father, though you probably guessed as much."

Heron nodded, reluctant to speak lest they push her into saying anything she'd regret.

"I was young when I came to Tharis, following my brother because I didn't want him to be alone and he needed to be somewhere other than home. It's a small village where we were born and grew up, much smaller than most of the villages we've passed by this progress and a speck compared to that." She waved at the distant city high above the forest of tents. "Everyone knows everyone's business and sticks their noses in all the time and he had to get away because . . . well, that's his business, but he did and I went with him because none of our other siblings were suitable, and maybe because I was curious about what things would be like somewhere else."

Heron had met many such over the years. They'd started that way too, although at some point in the long years of near-constant travel they'd discovered a longing to spend more time in one place. Oddly, despite the court's regular progress they still enjoyed several solid months in the summer and winter palaces—more than they'd had in Kitiva since they first started wandering.

"Aurel and I both found places in the palace, both in the kitchens at the start. He took to it but I didn't." She scowled, then shrugged. "It was longer than I like to remember before Desma caught me tidying the kitchen all the time. She wasn't palacekeeper for attendants, then, but on her way. But before then, I was lonely, and there was this other cook who showered me with flowers and special treats. He was also from a small town, near ours, and full of grand plans to rise to head chef or open a grand restaurant in the city or go back to his town and run the inn there."

A crash from nearby made them both jump and turn around, but then there was laughter and the sound of kissing from the other side of the next tent over.

"Big plans indeed." Heron did their best to ignore the soft sighs so close.

"And I'd be right by his side at the restaurant or the inn." Emmi heaved a very different sigh.

Heron returned to keeping their mouth shut, fingers knotted in their lap where Emmi couldn't see.

"He seemed to know what he wanted and how to get it, and I didn't. It took me so long to realize he was always making plans and never keeping them." Her gaze grew distant. "Always making promises and never keeping them either."

Heron's knuckles paled, fingers clenching ever tighter to keep from reaching out.

"By the time I did figure that out, Susa was on the way, so I hung on longer until she was born and a few weeks old and he started breaking promises to her also." Emmi sat straight, fists raised. "He'd be around for a week, helping take care of her, and then just when I thought he'd changed he'd vanish for a few days. Come back bearing a big bouquet of flowers and expect that to make everything right."

Here was one reason Amara—or was it Gisela?—had advised Heron not to give Emmi flowers when apologizing. They must have known or picked up something.

"He's better now." Emmi held her fists in front of her face. With a little laugh, she shook out her fingers, lips pulled sideways in a bitter smile. "His sister and her husband moved to Tharis and opened an inn, not him. He lives with them and works in it, runs the kitchens. He's good with Susa nowadays. Mostly keeps his promises to her. It probably helps that he only has to do that for three months out of the year, because the rest of the time we're away on progress or in Yaras."

"But you gave him time, attention, and chances, and he squandered them." Heron wouldn't make that mistake.

"I don't regret being with him, because I have Susa." Her smile turned genuine for a moment. "But I do wish I hadn't given him so very many chances."

"My errors of judgment are as many, but shorter. None lasted more than a few nights or a few weeks at best." Heron forced their hands to unclench. "I learned to listen when people told me they only wanted a little pleasure, or a taste of something different. Not well enough or fast enough, and I didn't apply the lessons far enough, but I learned."

"You don't need to tell me, not when it hurts." Emmi shifted around the trunk to settle close to Heron, near enough that they could feel warmth flowing from her body.

"The only hurt is in how long I took to learn." Heron shrugged. "I was a messenger, and Kitivan women knew that I'd be there and gone and coming back who-knew-when, so they never asked me for much more than a few nights, mostly for pleasure although one or two were upfront that they wouldn't mind seed for a child."

"Did you want more?"

"I learned not to hope at home quick enough, but it took time to realize how this was true elsewhere as well." They rubbed their aching hands, shaking away slivered memories of faces, voices, and touches that had turned into nothing more than hot air. Their memory keeper warmed against their chest, a visceral reminder of good faces, voices, and caring hearts. "Kitivan messengers never stay long outside the city, even if we have regular routes, which I sometimes did, and people liked that I would be leaving."

"I'm sorry." Emmi leaned close without touching, eyes wide and lips parted.

Heron swallowed, letting the rest of the tale spill out in a rush. "Then I became a princess, and I didn't understand Codaran customs. I thought that as I was in the same place, or at least with the same people in court, for longer, I might find someone for longer. But those that approached wanted the princess, not *me*."

"That happens a lot." Emmi filled a mug for them, hands steady this time.

"You may not know what you want yet, but I know something of what I want." Heron took the mug from them, careful not to brush fingers in the process no matter the strength of the desire. They sipped, then set it aside. "I wish for someone who sees more in me than a messenger or a princess, who cares for me as a person to keep around for long and longer."

"That makes sense, and I do see you as you, not just a princess." Emmi sat back, shoulders rounding. "But . . ."

Heron waited, until it was clear she lacked words or didn't want to let them fall. They guessed instead. "You need time?

"Yes." She nodded, relaxing with a slight sigh.

"Take it." They shrugged.

"Like that? So simple?" Emmi shook her head. "Is there nothing else you want?"

"I don't want to make conditions." Heron picked up their mug and drank deep.

"Then, not as a condition." Emmi bit her lip. "How can I know what you want, who you are, unless you tell me?"

Heron sat still for a few minutes, barely breathing, but she seemed earnest. Her gaze fixed on them, brows slightly lifted as if she knew she'd outlast them in waiting.

Might as well share a little. A hint. A possibility.

"When you're ready," Heron said, slow and braced for her to turn away. "I would appreciate some measure of touch."

They held out a hand.

Emmi stared at them, back and forth between face and hand. Licking her lips, she drew in a deep breath and rose to her feet.

"We can do better than that," she said, and opened her arms wide.

Heron stood, swaying and lightheaded. They moved no more than a few hairs closer with each shallow breath, braced against Emmi changing her mind. A chill filled them, melting under the heat pouring off her body as they at last stepped into her embrace. They tried not to hold on too hard, but it was so easy to get lost in the glory of arms wrapping around backs, a head resting against their chest, and their chin light against the top of her head.

To hold and be held by Emmi, which they'd desired for so long, because *she* wanted touch too.

Bliss.

❧ 13 ❧

E mmi braced for comments, criticism, and impertinent curiosity. At first, her changing situation went mostly unnoticed—helped, in no small part, by the weather.

The soft patter of rain on the tent woke Emmi. She huddled close to her snoring daughter, tugging her blanket closer about her neck for one moment. Then, shrugging off the indulgence, she dressed in the oldest, plainest, easiest-to-launder tunic she'd brought, with nothing more than rope at her waist and sandals at her feet. Susa slept on, mumbling and rolling over into Emmi's blanket.

Drizzle slicked Emmi's hair against her skull as soon as she left the tent. She bent and checked the earth, damp but not muddy yet. The rain must have just started.

She jumped as a young guard passed nearby, setting their fingers between their lips and issuing a loud whistle every few steps. Though she shouldn't have been surprised. The newness of the rain meant there was time to roust the progress and move on toward the next stop while the ground remained solid.

No one said anything or gave Emmi any sidelong glances, all too busy with the final tasks of getting on the road. Susa grumbled at having to rise early, but that was nothing new.

Two days' slog along tracks slowly turning mucky provided sufficient distraction from any curious minds and glancing eyes. Everyone had too much to do, busy grumbling, grumping, and knocking muck off feet, legs, hooves, and wheels. The order of walkers and wagons shifted around, ensuring no human or oxen spent too much time at the heel of the progress suffering through the churned-up earth. Even the Marchon took a turn following behind the rest without complaint, although his face made clear he enjoyed it no more than anyone else. Where he led, no one could refuse to follow although most did so with more grouching.

Susa enjoyed the rain at first. Along with the other children, she rejoiced at stripping off tunics and sandals as soon as the air had warmed enough. She darted around in her loin-wrap, which at least would make the eventual laundry easier. Three times the children started mud fights—the second half or three-quarters Susa's fault—and each instance the children's attendants squelched with increasing fierceness.

All too soon, Susa grew tired. When she learned she couldn't ride atop the carts, because the oxen had quite enough to pull the wagons through slick rutted earth, she clung to Emmi's hand and whined and dragged her feet.

Parents carrying younger, smaller children in slings or heaved over shoulders brought back keen memories of doing the same in previous years.

Alas, Emmi couldn't carry her. Susa had grown too big.

But Heron could. They only managed a short slog here and there—not a lot, but enough to reduce Susa's wails to occasional hiccups. When put back down, the girl learned to trudge along when tired, leaning against her mother and half asleep.

Yet another gift of Heron's time, attention, and energy that Emmi couldn't match.

Still, the look on their face when she touched their hand in thanks, or stole a moment at the end of the day for an embrace . . .

She'd do much to see that again. To know she'd caused it.

Not to mention how much comfort and ease she found in holding them and being held within their arms. The embraces had so little in common with when Emmi had hugged Aurel farewell, or clasped arms with family up north when she could steal away from Tharis to see them. Even the embraces with Su's father or the few others whom Emmi had lain with since paled in comparison.

First, none was as tall. Emmi's head barely reached Heron's shoulders. Although built long and lean, they managed to enfold her within their arms.

Equally, Emmi remembered no one else showing such clear enjoyment. With family, hugs were usually a quick squeeze of welcome or farewell, a physical way of saying we're glad you're here and we missed you or goodbye we will miss you. With lovers, hugs were never more than a step toward a desired end.

Heron hugged as though it was all they wanted. They didn't offer a quick squeeze or fingers digging and pulling, but rather a slow drawing close and closer until two bodies stood together from head to toe. Until their breaths matched. Emmi stood within their arms feeling the warmth around her, the solid muscles under her hands. How had she gone through so many years serving them without realizing how soft their skin, how supple their body? Standing there, it seemed as though if the rest of the world melted away and left only this, all would still be well.

The hugs helped her get through the days of rain and the equally awful trek across ground slowly drying after. Through the nights where it wasn't worth pitching wet tents, so everyone found as dry spots as they could. The luckiest stayed in an inn the day they were near a town, the second luckiest under the wagons, and everyone else, even princesses and compeers, wrapped themselves in cloaks or blankets and huddled under whatever shelter they could find: trees, mostly, this being a forested section, which meant steady drips but some protection.

Emmi had evidence the hugs helped Heron as well, as the news of their shifting relationship began to circle outward.

Of all people, the first clear response came from Emmi's fellow attendant, Fotis. Emmi hadn't had much to do with the eleee before the progress. Fotis was relatively new, hired to replace one of the many attendants who decided to stop traveling every year. The few times

Emmi had crossed paths with them, they'd seemed shy. Indeed, they'd hardly spoken above a whisper on the rare occasions they said anything.

That changed.

She wound up next to Fotis at a creek after the progress finally reached its next stop and could stay in place long enough to thoroughly dry out and clean off the mud. There was too much work for the launderers to handle it all, so Emmi and Fotis and other attendants helped.

Emmi and Fotis were given a towering pile of tunics and mantles, and the task of knocking off dried clods and determining which items required scrubbing or could do with a bit of sponging and wait until later. Farther down, others did the same with equally large piles while the launderers stripped to loincloths and waded into the center of the creek to duck and scrub. Several cats emerged from the city to line the far shore and observe the activity, but apart from the occasional meow they kept their distance. Newly aware of cats, after more exposure to Homer than she liked, Emmi noticed how the longest serving attendants seemed the least comfortable with the watching felines.

The newest and youngest, including Fotis, barely granted the creatures more than a glance.

Emmi wasn't afterward sure how long she worked with Fotis in mostly companionable silence. Quite a while, given the aches in her arms, shoulders, and back from bending over and back, before Fotis broke the quiet.

"They're happier now."

Emmi almost missed the words, as the young eleee had ducked their head as they spoke. "What?"

"The princess," Fotis said.

"Which?" She stood and braced her hands against the small of her back, stretching and getting ready for her personal life to be the subject of gossip.

Fotis lifted their head and gave her a look. They might be shy, but clearly weren't willing to play the game of Emmi not knowing who they meant.

Heat flooded Emmi's cheeks.

"They didn't ask you while you were serving them?" Fotis asked. "It's not clear from all that folks are . . ."

Of course people would jump to the conclusion that Heron might have done something wrong. Some people, but Fotis was brave enough to ask. Then again, Fotis served Heron as Emmi had, and perhaps had more personal worries.

"They did nothing inappropriate, said nothing wrong while I was their attendant." Emmi met Fotis's gaze straight on. "Nothing happened until after I stopped working for them."

Fotis nodded, grabbing a plain orange tunic and easing their fingers around clumps of mud hanging from the hem. "Whatever it is, it's made them happier. And you're happier too?"

"Yes." She glanced over at the path leading back to the new encampment, though she knew she wouldn't see Heron through the thick tree cover.

"I hope it lasts."

Many others echoed Fotis's sentiments one way or another. With the rain and mud increasingly behind them, and the earth drying out, Emmi's fellow attendants wished her well.

But also watched her more. Whispered when they thought she couldn't hear—they were right in that she never made out the words, even as she noted mouths moving when she wasn't around.

Comments and gossip stilling when she was. Sometimes she knew one or another swallowed something they would have said about Emmi, but other times the conversation until then had nothing to do with her or Heron that she could tell. The others had shifted to watching what they said around her, perhaps fearing she'd pass the wrong word along—and in doing so making a divide between Emmi and them.

The princesses and compeers also changed how they looked at, spoke with, and acted around her. She couldn't put her finger on the differences, only that they existed.

Worse were the kind of courtiers who'd never before paid Emmi any attention at all. First in drips and drabs and then more regularly, one or another would sidle up to her and pretend a friendship as an excuse.

One of the Marchon's aides stopped Emmi as she carried water for Zora—not noting when her arms started to tremble under the strain of holding the heavy jug—and paid her an unexpected compliment. In the next breath, Emmi was told to be sure that Heron didn't miss some gathering to be hosted by an elder of the city the progress camped near.

Several assistants to ministers or clerks tried to lure Emmi aside. Some weren't too bad, offering themselves to represent Emmi in negotiating a consortial contract with Heron, on the understanding they'd take a cut. Others seemed to think that if she was so desperate as to be interested in a princess—all that magic!—she'd be open to a wink and a snuggle on the side.

Serving Zora gave Emmi some relief from the courtiers' solicitations. None of them wanted to attract the wrong kind of attention from the royal compeer.

Furthermore, Zora made it quite clear from the start that she didn't care. The one time she said anything, it was in passing and left Emmi unclear whether Zora thought Emmi being with Heron was fine or hoped Emmi would either share Heron's tent or move hers near and thus be closer to Zora.

Or more accurately, the main Zora considered the matter none of her business. Emmi wasn't sure about the compeer's other selves.

One or more of them—Emmi still wasn't certain how many Zora held—regularly watched Emmi through narrowed eyes. Though the suspicion might be due to Emmi's helping Zora go through her prized possessions time after time rather than Emmi's relationship with Heron.

Alternatively, perhaps it arose because of the continuing interest between Homer and Susa, and the number of times Homer slipped away from Zora's tent to cuddle with Susa. This happened again and again, during the day and after the muddy days' passage it started taking place at night.

The first night camped outside the city, Emmi woke in the middle of the night choking on damp air, as the tent had yet to fully dry. Two round green spots glowed on the far side of Susa, cuddled in a curve rather than a compact ball.

The spots blinked, resolving into cat eyes. Homer hissed. Susa reached out in her sleep and petted the creature, curling toward him rather than toward her mother.

Emmi rose with caution when morning arrived, but the cat had gone.

Still, the cat and Susa's interest in each other made the girl a little easier to deal with.

The cat and Heron.

Even the children's palace attendants noticed Susa's preoccupation with both.

On the one hand, attendants and children became accustomed to Homer showing up on occasion. Usually he took a stroll around or lay in the sunniest spot to clean himself while the children played around. Most learned quickly not to draw close unless he purred. Susa reported proudly that he never clawed her, except when she stopped petting him before he was ready. Eventually, he would leave of his own accord. Or, equally often, Zora came to take him away or sent Emmi to do so.

On the other, when Emmi went to fetch Susa the second day into the new encampment, Lysia stopped her. Susa was playing on the far side, running among the rows of stalks left after the harvest. Laughing. Chasing another youngling, both full of joy and watched by two of the city cats clustered along the far end of the field while a third hunted nearby.

Likewise, so streaked with dirt and bits of bracken that Emmi felt clean in comparison although she wore a dark brown tunic, the better to hide stains.

"I hate to worry you," Lysia kept her voice low, no matter that no one was near enough to hear over the children's noise.

"Worry over what?" Emmi asked.

"Have you noticed that Susa talks about princess Heron all the time but doesn't mention her uncle-aunt? Not at all, since the first day we left Yaras." Lysia ticked off the days on her fingers, so many. "I've asked around, and no one has heard her say anything about Aurel."

"I hadn't thought." Emmi frowned, then shook her head. "I don't think I have either. Is it a problem?"

"I don't know. Consider how often she talked about him before we left. Not speaking doesn't mean she hasn't thought of him, even if every other word out of her mouth is Heron this, or Heron that." Lysia stared at Emmi, brows lifted.

"Of course." Emmi sighed. "Just as she used to talk about Aurel."

"That's what I'm wondering, if she's made a swap of sorts." Lysia shrugged, then leveled another even glance. "Have you told her how you feel about Heron?"

"I'm still figuring that out," Emmi said.

"I don't want to be telling you your business, but you might think of ways to let her know. Make it a secret, maybe? Something for her to hold close and treasure." Lysia waited until Emmi nodded before heading over to gather Susa.

Emmi led Susa on a circuitous path, stopping by the creek long enough to scrub Susa mostly clean. Warmed by the day's sun, the water around the girl turned muddy but quickly ran clear. Dirt lingered under the child's fingernails, but she'd just get more there the next day, so Emmi let that slide.

The girl was yawning, clearly tired, but mostly cooperative until Emmi brought her by the cook tents to grab a pastry each and spiced water for dinner.

"We need one for Heron." Susa tried to snatch a third, despite having one in each hand already—and a bite out of her own. Bright red juices dripped down her fingers, increasing the smell of berries and starmeg.

"Heron's in the city tonight, at a banquet with the Marchon. We're on our own." Emmi guided Susa firmly away.

Her reward was grumbling and whining all the way back to their tent.

Wouldn't Heron come see them after the banquet?

No it would be too late.

Couldn't they go to the banquet?

No, they weren't invited.

How about sneaking in?

No, they're not rude enough to stick their noses where they aren't wanted, and besides someone needed to go to bed.

Can they go get Homer, since the cat wasn't in sight hanging around the tent?

No, it should be Homer's choice whether to visit them or not.

Every time Emmi thought the matter settled, Susa came up with another variation on the same theme. No, no, no, dropped off Emmi's tongue until she was quite sick of the word.

Susa's struggles to change into her night tunic allowed Emmi a little time to eat her pastry in a few bites, washed down with spiced water. The child hung her play tunic over a branch arcing from a nearby tree, the wet fabric hardly flapping in the breeze. Emmi fixed it in place with a length of rope wrapped around fabric and wood. Dipping in the creek had left the cloth mostly clean and smelling of watery green things.

Just as a hint of sun and autumn leaves clung to Susa's night tunic after hanging out all day. Emmi settled down in the tent, rolling her sweet-smelling daughter into a blanket.

"Story time?" Susa laid her head in her mother's lap.

"Maybe." Emmi stroked damp curls from the girl's forehead. "Do you miss uncle-aunt?"

Susa turned her face against her mother's belly, muffling her words. "He should've come with us."

"I miss him, too, but we'll see him next summer." Emmi kept stroking, alternating between watching her daughter and glancing through the open tent door at the fading light. Faint glows began to mark the places where baskets of luminescent mosses marked paths through the tents. "You'll see your father soon!"

Emmi might not look forward to that, but she was rewarded with a wiggle from Susa. The girl rolled onto her back.

"Will Heron still come for dinner when I'm with father? They'll know where he lives?"

The mere idea unsettled Emmi, but it was highly unlikely. Heron and her former lover had so little in common. "Heron may not visit you when you stay with your father. But you can come to the palace to see them and me."

"Heron shouldn't be at palace." Susa frowned, hands curling into fists and lips trembling "They can stay with me!"

Heron or uncle-aunt? Little difference in this. Emmi stroked Susa until the girl's hands unclenched. Just one more in a series of lessons about the ways life didn't go the way a person wanted because they wanted it.

Weary though she was, Susa didn't go to sleep. She kept mumbling about wishing Heron would come from the banquet and tell her a story.

Emmi lay down on her blanket, face to face with her daughter. Her feet poked out the tent door where the breeze chilled her toes. "You know Heron is my . . . friend, too."

Susa shrugged.

"I'll always be your mother and they'll always be your friend, but Heron and I are getting to know each other better." Emmi combed her fingers through Susa's hair.

"They're my friend first." The girl drew back, then leaned into the caress. "But they can be yours too."

"We might not be the same kind of friends."

Susa yawned and rolled over, pulling her blanket around her. She didn't seem upset. Emmi clung to that as she finished getting herself ready for bed. No need to push too far too fast.

"They may be your friend first," Emmi whispered. "But they're becoming my special friend."

Her daughter made no response.

＃ 14 ＃

"Are people acting oddly around you?"

Heron jerked at the question. They'd gotten so comfortable, leaning back against a tree near Emmi's tent. The sun had almost set, streaking the sky with lavender and pink visible through the branches of the trees marking the line between fields. The fading light left the air cooling, but Heron was warm. Emmi sat on their lap and leaned against their chest, dressed in a lovely blue tunic still colorful despite ample wear and washing. A simple silver mantle draped around Heron's shoulders over their dark green tunic. Three layers of cloth between them—just enough and too much.

Susa snored softly in the tent nearby, finally, after increased yawning through three stories.

Despite the growing shadows, Heron could still see Emmi's features and even some of Susa's in the starlight and distant mossy glows. Sonnewood clung to Emmi, particularly her hands, but the breeze whisked enough away to leave only a trace.

The note in Emmi's voice warned Heron the question wasn't idle. Soft murmurs floated from nearby tents. Most of the people Heron knew by sight at best, but Emmi knew them all—and most of those with whom Heron usually talked and ate. Only natural and to be expected, as a function of Emmi having tended Heron's rooms and things for so long. Yet also perhaps part of the natures of their positions at court.

"Are people here treating you differently?" Heron asked. "Or those over where my tent is?" The other princesses and the compeers.

"It seems like everyone's got an opinion about us, even if only a few say anything to my face." Emmi sighed, tucking her head closer to Heron's shoulder.

"Is this good or bad?

"Not either. I don't know." She sat up, leaving a cooling spot behind, discomfort clear on her face. "I got a taste of what you might've meant when you said people saw you as a princess, not as you."

Heron tensed, arms pinning close against their sides. Their jaw clenched, air whistling as they drew in a tight breath.

"No, it wasn't bad, not really." She settled back against them, if not cuddled so close as before. "Just folk seeing me as a way to get things to you, or wanting me to ask things of you and thinking all they have to do is dangle a sparkle or something at me to get me to agree."

Nearly every city and country Heron had traveled through tried to discourage and root out bribery. It flourished regardless. Codaros had less than some places, but not none. "Didn't anyone ever do that when you tended me?"

They held their breath against the answer, hoping she hadn't been pestered without their noticing.

"It's against the rules." Emmi shook her head, tilting her head to give him a sideways smile. "We'd be rolled out on our shoulders if we were caught, and everyone knows that."

"Everyone," Heron said.

"You didn't?" Emmi sat up again, the movement a second time chilling Heron's chest where she'd rested her head.

"I don't remember being told as much, only not to abuse power." They'd been told so many things those first, confusing days after being presented as a princess. Maybe someone had mentioned the matter, and they'd let it go.

"That's one way, by respecting attendants and not asking them to do things they shouldn't, which you never did." Emmi said.

"Unless I didn't know any better."

"You didn't." A statement this time, much different from her earlier surprise.

Heron leaned forward, burying their head against Emmi's neck for a moment. Her certainty flooded them with warmth. Eyes damp, they sat back ready to return to the earlier matter—or problem. "Do you mind much people changing how they are around you?"

"Most folk aren't saying anything to me directly, it's more in what they're not saying." Emmi shrugged. "The way conversations halt and then change when I pass by, and there's maybe gossip they're not sharing when I'm around anymore. It's no more than to be expected, really. Is that how they are with you?"

"I'm not sure how much I'd notice people not saying things," Heron said. "And I don't have to guess what most of the princesses and compeers are thinking, because they've all tracked me down one way or another to tell me."

"They did?" Emmi's face was a study in shadow and confusion.

"Amara first."

Heron had risen early to join the retired princess in sun stretches after the long rainy, muddy trek. Other princesses and compeers slept in, still recovering from slogging along wretched tracks. Some snored, one mumbled in their sleep, but none stepped into the open square outlined by the princess and compeer's tents. It was just the two of them in loose, light tunics. They lifted their hands and stretched their bodies in silence as they traced the sun's arc.

But after the last deep bend, Amara turned to Heron. Despite the layer of sweat coating her skin, with her arms crossed over her chest and head tilted to one side she assumed a stern expression.

"Emmi's going to lengths for you, so you had better be clear with her what you want and what you don't."

Heron had nodded, unsure how to respond.

She sniffed. "And it wouldn't hurt you to find someone to help you learn about Codaran courting customs, all ten million of them, but that someone can't be me."

Emmi chuckled when Heron recounted Amara's admonition. "I asked Amara about Kitivan courting customs."

"Well she wasn't quite as right as she might have thought." Heron frowned. Amara had left Emmi with the notion that Kitivans were extremely formal, which still irked. Even compared with the more lax Codarans, they were not. More formal, yes, but not to such extremes. "Perhaps I can find someone more familiar with what you're looking for?" Several Kitivan traders frequented Tharis, so Heron could approach one of them.

"I'll think about it." Emmi pressed her hands together. "Who else talked to you?"

"Melite offered to be a go-between."

"Melite?" Emmi looked puzzled, then nodded. "She's from midway between Yaras and Tharis. I didn't know they still used go-betweens. I've heard of them in stories, but that's not something I'm used to."

Heron kept their mouth shut, glad Emmi hadn't embraced the notion of bringing someone else into their negotiations. The two of them, plus any advisers, were more than enough.

"Is that all?" Emmi asked.

"Gisela tracked me down earlier today, and I mean tracked, because I was over in the city looking at the streets where they hold their autumn market."

Heron had wandered along a well-trodden street of cobblestones where a few traders had already begun selecting spots and parking their wagons, with many more expected in the next day or two. The traders called to each other, bantering welcomes and mock disparagement of each others' goods. Most of the traders' wagons bore elaborate painted decorations showcasing what they sold. One in particular had caught Heron's eye, with an array of toys in lurid colors. Bright purple and green balls. Miniature versions of the trader's wagons, some pulled by wooden people and others by oxen or donkeys. More animals, with their feet set on wheels so they could be pulled around. The activity had drawn the attention of a dozen or more cats, mostly observing from walls and rooftops.

The notion of walking through the market with Emmi and Susa, and seeing what caught their eyes, had distracted Heron to the point they nearly ran into the toy wagon proprietor.

"Well, I'll be, I know that kind of lankiness and ease of moving." Under a broad-brimmed hat, the trader stroked a gray-streaked beard with a deep bronze-toned hand. "You'll be Stork's kin, yes?"

"Stork, yes." Heron stopped of a sudden, one foot flat on an even cobblestone and the other angled down into the dip between stones. "My uncle."

"Will he be coming to the market soonish?" The trader asked. "He wasn't being sure when last I saw him, though he swore he'd make it as he'd plans for trading—and he knows I promised on being here with more of the sets of cards he was wanting."

"I saw him awhile back, but I don't know where he was headed then." Heron shrugged. "I'm sorry."

Before the trader could push or pry, two whirlwinds blew to Heron's side. Gisela and Stevan, both clad as simply as Heron.

"You'll excuse us, but we have need of Heron." Gisela charmed the trader with a smile as Stevan hustled Heron off to a vacant alley. Little more than a dip between stone-work buildings, it offered privacy if they kept their voices down.

"You followed me here?" Heron shook their head. "What couldn't wait until I got back to the camp?"

"Gisela heard something she wanted to learn the truth of." Stevan smiled. "It wasn't hard to find you."

Heron sighed. It wouldn't be, for Stevan. A born compeer, his magic let him match princesses in the Dance—or find anyone within the palace, or a city.

Gisela stomped over after having appeased the trader, blocking the entrance to the alley. Her posture resembled Amara's, down to the line of her arms across her chest. "Are you really courting with Emmi?"

"You had to come find me to ask that?"

"I wanted to know straight, and who better from than you." Gisela scowled. "You haven't answered the question."

"And I won't." Heron frowned back. "If we are, that's our business,"

Gisela glanced past Heron at Stevan. She hadn't been at court long, but Stevan had served as a low-level clerk of some kind before the

Terparchon realized his power and snapped him up to Dance, and to partner Gisela.

"That means they are," Stevan said.

"Oh good! That's wonderful." The scowl dropped off Gisela's face and she darted in to give Heron a quick hug.

Heron froze. Her touch was very different from Emmi's—light and friendly, little more than the press of hands against their back and then she moved back to lean against Stevan. Still, a welcome reminder that not everyone at court, or everyone in Codaros, avoided touch.

Stevan coughed and shrugged, giving Gisela an indulgent smile.

"Oh, I forgot." Gisela threw up her hands. "Court is so strange about so many things. Still, even I could see that you're lonely and that Emmi had a softer look in her eye whenever she gazed at you. The elders of my village would say you each had aches that might fit fine together, all the better to keep your toes warm."

Emmi laughed again, bringing Heron back to the delight of the present and her body nestled against them instead of Gisela's fast clasp. A few streaks of lavender remained, but the sky was slowly turning ever-deeper shades of blue.

"Aches fitting together?" Emmi shook her head. "Still, that's sweet of her."

Heron's arms wrapped loosely around Emmi, leaving them not lonely in the slightest. They could just stay here all night without the need to leave, if only they could, and escape Stork's request hanging over them.

"Was Gisela the last?"

"Other than Zora, who doesn't care." Heron eased Emmi to slide down and lean against them so that they could rest their chin atop her hair. All the better to keep her from studying their face. Even with the fall of night, the stars offered enough light to see expressions this close.

"She said that to me, too, while holding the cat who was glaring at me." Emmi shivered.

"She wasn't holding the cat with me."

Zora had stood in front of her tent when she made the statement. A small trunk sat near the door, half-packed with odd-shaped items each wrapped in cloth. The remaining contents were spread around. A few carved figures rested face-down on a length of yellow silk. An ugly white stone pitted with gray marks sat nearby on a round of blue linen. Zora positioned herself between them and Heron as though defending her possessions. Her arms hugged a bound volume against her chest as she stared over it at Heron.

They responded to her words appropriately, or so they thought, for they couldn't recall what they said even as much as a moment later—because the book matched the description they'd been given of the often-missing compendium of Dances.

If so, it was within their reach, but nothing they could touch without antagonizing Zora, who made a bad enemy.

"Just promise me the Marchon hasn't said anything." Emmi's voice was partly muffled, buried against Heron's chest.

"I'm sure someone's told him, but I walked in and out of the banquet last night within arms' reach of him, and he said nothing. I don't expect him to either. Neither he nor the Terparchon have made any noises about princesses or compeers partnering with anyone in all the years I've been a princess." All five, but they were enough.

"Not even their children's pairings." Emmi nodded. "It's good to know we aren't breaking the tradition with . . . whatever we are or will become."

Her body stiffened. Heron let their arms fall away, so she might move or withdraw as she chose. The night wind twisted around them, chilling skin through cloth save where they remained close together.

Emmi sat back, face lifting to meet his gaze. "What are we becoming?"

Starlight allowed Heron to note the worry on her face matching the note in her voice and the stiffness to her shoulders.

"Is rushing part of Codaran courting customs?" they asked.

"I don't understand."

"You're going fast, is that necessary?" Heron wanted every mote of time they could have with her, even if this was all it was. Courting was a process, but Emmi seemed to consider it something to be done even though that didn't seem to make her happy.

"Don't you want to know?" A hard sound, half-cough and half-laugh escaped her. "Kitivans are never in a hurry?"

"Oh, we're often in a hurry." Heron rubbed a hand across their forehead, slicking damp hairs to the side. "If this were only desire for bodily pleasure we might have slaked it by now, Kitivans or Codarans or whoever. But I want more, and more won't go bad for taking time to enjoy the process—and to be sure."

15

Emmi shivered. Heron's arms held her close, cradling her. If asked, she'd have guessed that sitting on Heron's lap while they leaned against a tree would mean discomfort and boniness, but instead their legs supported her below and their chest offered a luxurious pillow to rest against. Warmth permeated her whole body, strongest where their bodies met. The darkening twilight hid most of their expression from her, but the bits of light from stars and moss baskets captured the basic lines of Heron's face as they gazed down at her.

A sharp, earthy scent blew away the last haze of sonnewood hanging about her, replacing it with an aroma reminiscent of the first moments of rainfall: crisp, clear, and comforting. The rest of the world faded away in contrast, leaving only Heron and Emmi and a rising flurry of desire fed by their low-whispered determination not to move too fast.

Fast? Heron and Emmi had done everything slow to this point. Spent years looking and thinking with never a touch. So much unspoken interest and longing pent up, that even this middling shift to touch, to hold, ranked as an immense change.

A welcome one.

Still, Emmi equally appreciated Heron's willingness to take things slow and not rush.

Emmi had rushed before. A flurry of desires and glances across a hot kitchen led within a moon to bodies thrashing in bed, and then into clashes and bitter disappointment.

And Susa, which more than balanced it all out.

Still, surely there was room to move a little faster without rushing?

Except, the slowness was Emmi's doing. Heron had stated what they wanted: someone who saw all of them, wanted to be with them for themselves rather than parts of them that might come and go such as rank and position.

What did Emmi see when she looked at them?

A source of mess, impossible not to consider after the years she'd spent tending them. Never too much, but always they left something for her to tidy, now for Fotis.

Cautious about their clothing always, and careful to note rents and tears in need of mending, likely from years of traveling on their own, and having to make do with only as much as they could carry. This also explained the relative lack of stuff in their rooms, whether at the summer or winter palace. They seemed always ready to move on— braced against the necessity—even as they clearly enjoyed staying in one place for moons at a time.

Then there was the stranger-turned friend who'd traded stories about their home and the many places they'd been for Emmi's stories and advice about becoming Codaran.

Friend who became ever closer, as exchanges of stories and advice turned into all manner of conversations over the years.

The princess whom she'd seen and admired from a distance dancing at court events. She'd rarely seen them Dance until recently, but they were so clearly made for Dance magic. They'd been so beautiful in the village: their every motion filled with grace, purpose, and power.

Emmi had been unable to look away. Heron's every move revealed such energy and fire contained within their long, lean body, something they'd hidden otherwise behind a placid expression except for the occasions when she'd caught hints of desire in their eyes.

Only to turn away.

No longer.

She wanted the friend and confidant, the Dancing princess, and the fire and longing so long banked within them.

Now she let herself see how Heron quivered when their fingers brushed hers, the surprise and delight when the two joined in an embrace, and how their body always leaned toward her for a moment when a hug ended, as if trying to hold on a little longer.

She shifted, pulling away from their chest and slipping off their lap.

Heron's grasp tightened for a moment, as they startled, but in the next breath they let go. Their hands softly brushed Emmi's sides as she pulled back.

They remained in place, leaning against the tree with hands fisted and pressed against their belly. Perhaps the better to not reach after her?

She knelt opposite them. Close, with knees almost touching their legs and only enough room between for thin layers of cloth. Just enough stars shone from behind to let her note the gleam in Heron's eyes, the way their chest heaved and stilled as they caught their breath, and the angle of their head leaning toward her.

Emmi leaned forward, watching them the whole time. Her skin shimmered in the ray of starlight as she reached for them—hand moving with such slow deliberation her muscles trembled, all so that Heron could avoid her touch if they wished.

Heron remained still. They barely seemed to breathe as she cupped their cheek. The skin was warm and smooth despite the faintest prickle of hair.

"This"—Emmi rubbed her thumb along Heron's cheekbone— "means a lot to you."

"Yes." They shivered. Mirroring her slowness, they laid a hand over hers. They didn't press or push. Their fingers were cooler than their face, but her hand flared with heat pouring up her arm and rippling through her.

"Why? It's special, but seems more to you." She kept caressing their face with her thumb, noting the shift as they swallowed hard.

"You have Susa and your family in the north and your brother in the south to hold, hug, touch."

"While you have no one here." Curving her other hand around their other cheek, she jerked as the energy coursing through her body doubled. She'd known they were alone, lonely, but not realized how it extended to the simplest elements of life, of living and moving through a world without people to caress and be caressed by.

"Not for this." They laid their other hand atop hers, mimicking the movement of her thumbs but stroking the backs of her hands. "My family, when I was growing up, everyone touched all the time. Pats, taps, shoulders brushing. Parents, siblings, uncles, aunts, cousins, everyone. Sometimes slaps or pinches when I did something wrong, which was often enough especially when I was little, and when it became clearer that I didn't fit in, though at first it wasn't for a lack of trying no matter how often accused of that."

"They hurt you?" Emmi drew back, but torso only. Her arms straightened, as she couldn't bring herself to pull her hands away.

"It's hard to explain, they did and they didn't." Heron sighed, slipping their fingers under Emmi's hands. In a series of smooth movements she couldn't quite track, they managed to shift from pressing her hands against their face to entwined hands and brushing foreheads. "Touch was—is—how we showed love, and how we tried to help people back on the way if they started to go off. They don't understand me, never did, and were happy enough to see me taken on as a messenger, but also always delighted when I came back to visit no matter how long."

"Do they love you for who you are?" Emmi pulled away, slapping her hands against her face as she realized what she'd asked.

"They may not see me for all of who I am, but they love regardless." Heron shrugged, tears glittering in their eyes. "Enough to let me go to find other places I fit better, even as they hope that I'll see sense —their sense—and come home someday."

"I can see doing that for Susa, loving her enough to let go." More words bubbled up, wishes to be big enough to accept whatever Susa might make of herself. She swallowed them, unwilling to cast shadow on Heron's tenderness for their family.

"You love Susa. It's so clear, she has to see it."

"Except when she doesn't want to." Emmi chuckled, but Heron's reassurance brought back her earlier thoughts about seeing them clearly. What did they see when they looked at her? But it was only fair to offer her side first. Leaning back toward them, this time with her hands pressing against her rapidly thumping chest, she asked "Do you know what I see when I look at you?"

They spoke, at least their mouth moved, but the shadows drank whatever words Emmi might have read in sun. The air between her and Heron vibrated, as though their own personal breeze wreathed around them.

"I see someone who became a friend when I wasn't expecting it. A source of fascinating stories and tales of far-off places I'll never see. A princess who was made to Dance, so glorious in movement that you take my breath away." Bit by bit she angled closer, drawn to the warmth and energy pouring off them. "Someone I'm daring to love."

"I see a mother filled with care," Heron nearly breathed their words into her mouth, as she drank in their response. "A devoted tidier who can laugh and joke as she cleans and leaves everything better for her having been there. Someone who I always want to spend more time around, would do anything for, spill any secret. Who I've been longing to kiss."

Even as they said the word, Emmi closed the last gasp of space between them.

Lips met. Touched. Awkward for a moment, until Heron rose onto their knees. Their shoulders rounded so their mouth meshed with Emmi's at a better angle.

Over and over they kissed. Soft, whispering slips of lips across lips. The brush of tongue. Bodies inched closer, hands wrapping around backs in a familiar hug made more by lips feeding desire that flared in every mote of Emmi's body.

Until broken by a sudden scream.

"No!"

Emmi rocked, chilled as she pulled away. Longing to remain in Heron's embrace warred with recognition of the surprise and anger in

Susa's voice. One hand stroking down Heron's arm, Emmi turned and tried to shape trembling lips into a smile. "Did you have a bad dream?"

Susa crawled out of tent, chin quivering and shaking her head. Her sleep tunic hung down past her knees, the loose fabric wrinkled and partially covered with cat hairs. The shadows swallowed most of her expression, and the arm's length distance still more—even so, Emmi read loss and loneliness on her daughter's face.

"You were—" Susa sniffed, pointing at Heron. "You're *my* friend."

"I still am," Heron said.

"They are." Emmi's legs swayed as she stood. Heron rose behind her, bracing her. "They're my friend, too, just a different kind."

"You're not uncle-aunt, you're not my friend." Susa drew inward, hands crossing over her chest. "You just wanted me to like you so my mother would. So she'd like you better."

"No, nothing could ever do that." Emmi stumbled forward with arms open, but Susa backed away.

"Don't touch me!"

Rocking, Emmi stopped in her tracks, hands still extended. She dropped to one knee to be level with her daughter. "Susa—"

Even as the name left Emmi's mouth, the girl turned. She snatched a lump of cloth, her blanket or something, from inside the tent. With a flick of her heels, she ran off into the wood and vanished in the darkness.

16

“**S**usa?”

Heron's arm ached from holding a moss basket high. The circle of soft green light around them only made the shadows deeper in contrast. The warmth, light, and muted bustle of camp lay behind. A stretch of empty land, field let go fallow, separated camp from the line of trees marking boundaries between fields. On the other side, guards patrolled with their own lights. Golden flashes denoted their passage.

Another sphere of green light with a small, thin form at the center ran from guard to guard. Emmi's voice carried across the emptiness, high and strained as she asked if they'd seen her daughter.

The cool breeze stole their answers, but her fevered movement told the tale.

“Susa!”

A half-dozen voices echoed the call as Emmi's tent neighbors spread out with still more baskets raised high. So many points of light, so many shadows—alas, mostly flat.

No sign of a young girl anywhere.

Emmi reached the far end of the field, lengths from her tent, then turned around and started back along the line of sentries.

Another bobbing point of green intercepted her and drew her back. Heron searched the shadows until the two meshed circles of light approached him. An elder with light hair had an arm slung around Emmi's shoulder.

"Take her back," the elder said, waving at Heron to come closer. "Best she stay at her tent, where any news can find her."

"But—" Emmi shifted, nearly slipping from the woman's light touch.

"No, you be there when we find her, so there's no time wasted bringing the two of you together." The elder nudged Emmi closer to Heron.

"I'll take you there." Heron's hand shook as they extended it. They were cold, but Emmi's fingers near ice to the touch when she slipped her hand in theirs—and eased a thousandth of the dread rippling through them.

"You won't stop looking?" Emmi asked the elder, curled into Heron's shoulder and face tinged with green that wasn't solely due to the moss light.

"They won't." Heron told her over and over as they guided her back through the maze.

Voices called encouragement as they passed by, hands reaching out to tug at Emmi's hem though no one touched her. The signs of caring eased the greenish cast of her skin, but she clung to Heron as though needing something, someone, to hold onto.

If not Susa, then him.

Another elder was at Emmi and Susa's tent site, tidying. Brushing away the layers of dust that spoke of the small crowd that had gathered and then dispersed in search of the girl. A hint of spice mingled with earth in the air, rising from a pitcher of fresh, hot spiced water the elder must have fetched.

"Oh, Lysia, have you seen—" Emmi let go of Heron to lurch forward.

"Don't I wish it," Lysia said. "Here, have a seat and a drink to take away the chill, then you can get your mind in order to think where Susa might've gone."

"We've already looked everywhere." Emmi dropped onto a pile of cloth near the edge of the tent.

"We'll find her." Heron squatted next to her, legs aching not from the position but the scratches they'd gotten while stumbling through the field in the dark. They wrapped hands around a warm mug Lysia handed them, and held it to Emmi's lips.

Her fingers trembled as she tried to hold it. Heron laid theirs over hers, feeling warmth seep from clay to skin as she drank.

They shifted back when she pushed cup away, falling onto their backside. Lysia was there, ready to take the mug and fill it again.

But Emmi was trying to rise. Her arms wouldn't hold her at first—then she scrabbled her hands around the cloth beneath her.

"This is Susa's blanket." Emmi rubbed her cheek against it, then turned her shadowed face toward Heron. "She didn't take it?"

"Not if you're holding it," Heron said.

"She grabbed something when she left. I thought it was her blanket." Emmi's hands busily folded the cloth and stroked away wrinkles, although her gaze was distant.

"She had something lumpy." Heron tried to remember. "A tunic?"

Whirling around, Emmi darted into the tent. After several thumps and bumps and grunts, she emerged gray-faced. "A pair of Susa's sandals are missing, and her thickest mantle."

"Then she may not be running to hide, but running away?" Lysia crouched near Emmi, peering into the tent.

"But where . . . to Aurel?" Emmi shivered. "We're too far from Yaris!"

"Would she know that?" Lysia asked.

The woman seemed to know Susa as well as Emmi, better than Heron for all they'd spent time with the child. They pushed to their feet, hovering a few steps back but unsure of what best to do to help.

"The guards hadn't seen her, so she can't have left the camp." Emmi clapped hands against her mouth. "Unless they could miss one small girl in the dark."

"Maybe the earth hasn't dried and we'll find her footsteps at first light." Lysia glanced up. The sky remained dark with no hint of light, but all the same she said, "it should be day soon enough."

The mention of footsteps made Heron stiffen. They didn't have to wait for light. "Stevan should be able to find her. He's a born compeer and can track footsteps. I'll get him."

Emmi nodded, though Heron wasn't certain she understood. Lysia did, and waved for them to go. "I'll stay with her," she promised.

Off Heron went, basket held high again. They darted between tents as they headed for the circular camp of princesses and compeers, wishing for the first time they had compeer magic and could be of more assistance.

How could a child run far so fast?

Soft noises from inside Gisela and Stevan's tent suggested they cuddled together against the night's cool. Heron kept a reasonable distance as they called for Stevan.

His head and bare shoulders popped out of the tent doorway, look of annoyance clear in the green moss light. "What is it?"

"There's a child missing," Heron said. "We need help finding her."

"A child?" Gisela stepped out in a hastily donned tunic, hair loose and tangled.

"Emmi's daughter, Susa. She's run away, or so we think," Heron said.

One look from Gisela, and Stevan drew in a hissed breath. He grimaced, but nodded. "I'll try."

Ducking back inside, he emerged in a rumpled tunic, with sandals in either hand and sashes looped around his neck. "Lead the way," he said as he passed a pair of sandals to Gisela and shoved his feet into the other.

Stevan was hot on Heron's heels as they headed back, breath warming their neck. Gisela trailed along behind, an additional set of footsteps thudding on the earth.

"I don't think I've ever met Emmi's daughter," Stevan said. "Susa is it?"

"Does that make a difference?" Heron asked, glancing over their shoulder in time to catch a grimace on Stevan's face.

"It'll make things harder."

As they approached Emmi's tentsite, there was no missing the voices calling for Susa in the distance. Several of her neighbors hovered near, without venturing into the oval area before the tent.

Just as well. Emmi was on her knees in the tent tossing things out. A pile of tunics and mantles and sandals formed odd shadows next to the bulk of a wicker trunk.

Backing out, she rose and kicked the pile. Instead of bending to neaten them, she wrapped her arms around her shoulders. Lysia hovered near.

Shaking, Emmi glanced at Heron. Her teeth flashed in the light as she bit her lip. "Susa took her sandals, two pairs, and a second tunic and a mantle. She had to have them ready to grab. She was planning to leave!"

"That doesn't mean she truly meant to run away," Lysis said. "She might have been preparing just in case, without really meaning to leave. Children often flee just far enough to be easily found."

"Children were always running away from Foleilion and rarely made it farther than the second stand of trees." Gisela hurried over to Emmi, pausing for a moment before hugging her. Emmi stiffened then slithered down into a heap on the ground.

"I missed it all. I was so busy thinking of . . ." She turned to Heron again, devastation in her glance.

Maybe Susa hadn't meant to go, but when she'd found Heron and Emmi kissing, she'd changed her mind?

Heron moved closer to offer comfort, but Emmi shrank away. They settled an arm's length back, close enough to reach if Emmi wanted.

Perhaps she blamed them?

Stevan coughed and shifted around Heron to crouch next to Emmi. "Heron asked me to see if I can find your daughter."

"Can you?" she asked.

"I can try, but it won't be easy." Stevan coughed again. "Does your daughter share your blood?"

"Yes, I gave birth to her," Emmi said.

Heron huddled as close as Emmi allowed. They listened to Stevan's soft questions and Emmi's shaky answers, all the while searching the shadows and circles of light in faint hope that Susa had reconsidered and returned.

Only to spy a very different figure stalking into the tentsite.

Zora marched right up to Emmi, the silver trim on her long blue mantle sparkling in the light. Her hands held something dark in front of her mantle and light-blue tunic. She let go and it landed with a heavy thud, proving to be Homer's basket.

Hands on her hips, she glared at Stevan, still crouched in front of Emmi, but ignored the rest. "You're searching for the missing child, are you?"

"Yes." Stevan stood.

"Well you can find Homer, too. She's stolen him!"

"What?" Heron rose, hovering over Emmi.

"How do you know?" Stevan asked.

Zora pointed at the basket. "He always sleeps here, except when he sneaks off to be with that girl, and where is he now?" Her head turned this way and that, although she didn't seem to truly look. "Nowhere here. Off with that thief, instead."

As Zora ordered Stevan to search for Homer, offering all manner of suggestions as to where the cat and girl might have got to, Heron started tidying Emmi's things.

Lysia and Gisela hovered near Emmi. Lysia didn't touch Emmi. Gisela offered a tentative squeeze of Emmi's shoulder, stopping when Emmi shivered.

Even given how little Codarans touched, that seemed extreme, and hard on Emmi. Touch meant different things to her than to Heron, but in times of hardship it offered comfort.

They picked up Emmi's half-full mug of cooling spiced water and knelt next to Emmi, offering it to her.

"If the cat did run off with Susa, then she's not alone," Heron said, leaving unsaid that neither was Emmi. Many people had gathered and gone out to search or clustered near to keep her company.

Heron teetered, wishing both to race off and join the searchers and wanting to remain to help Emmi keep hope alive.

"The cat running off with her, not the other way around?" Emmi asked, a hint of color in her cheeks. She took the mug, downed the water, and then latched onto Heron's hand. Her fingers had gone so cold no wonder she shivered. They wrapped a blanket around her shoulders, and their arms over that.

And waited with her through the dark of night.

$\mathfrak{F}$ I7 $\mathfrak{F}$

How much had Emmi missed?

She huddled between Heron and the tent pole. Layers of cloth—a blanket, Heron's mantle—warmed her body but failed to touch the chill deep within. Feet pressed against the cooling earth. Hands rubbed together. Heron's arm sometimes wrapped around her waist drawing her close. All in vain, for each thing seemed separate and strange.

Deep night had fallen. Clouds and sky formed a dark mass overhead, save a thin curve of the moon. Green light from moss baskets placed around—nine times the usual allotment—filled the area with light but did not let Emmi mistake the strangeness.

Quiet, too, had fallen. The calls for Susa had grown farther and farther away, finally dissolving under the press of distance. Searchers still looked, still called. She believed that, but without hearing belief had less force.

Occasional snores or snorts came from nearby tents. Normal sounds—at least someone, somewhere, could sleep.

Emmi longed to be out searching—to be doing *something*. Remaining here made sense. When Susa was found, for she would accept nothing but *when*, the news would come fastest if the finders knew where she was.

Doing nothing. Waiting. Hoping.

Fearing.

Stevan sat over by the tree where Heron and Emmi had stood—how many hours earlier?

He made a very different picture. A single body instead of two, seated rather than standing, and head hunched in his heads. He'd lifted it a while back and said he thought he might have found which way she went. South, but not west, and not quite on a road, there was a sense of a child passing with a cat.

Since then?

Nothing.

Gisela and Lysia remained near, keeping Emmi company. They'd brought blankets from somewhere and wrapped up as they leaned against each other. Whether they slept or waked, she wasn't sure, but they did so in silence.

Zora had left.

The quiet was good, because earlier every new arrival meant repeating the story, the few details, the little known information yet again until Emmi had wanted to scream that she knew it all and couldn't they just find Susa?

But the silence was also bad, because it left Emmi alone with her worries, her questions, and her guilt.

She'd missed so much. Hadn't seen Susa was unhappy to the point of wanting to leave. Overlooked all the signs of plotting, of Susa tying her extra clothes and sandals up, of grabbing the cat.

Instead of worrying and wondering about Susa, Emmi had worried and wondered about Heron.

"It's not your fault." Heron shook their head and rolled their shoulders.

"How do you know I was thinking that?" Emmi huddled deeper into the wraps, turning her head. They loomed above her even seated, the light from the basket glowing up and making their lips easy to see but their eyes into dark pits.

"I guessed, based on your expression," Heron said. "Which is the same as the last time."

Was this Emmi's third or seventh time fretting over her responsibility? It didn't matter, the core truths remained. "I just can't . . . I didn't see, didn't realize. I thought she was okay leaving Aurel and coming with me on progress."

"Susa might have thought twice about running if she hadn't been startled. She'll likely turn around and come back."

"If she doesn't get lost in the woods." Emmi stopped rubbing her hands and clenched them instead.

"Stevan will find her." Heron moved slowly as they wrapped their hands around hers, giving her a chance to pull away. Wanting the warmth, the touch, the comfort, she didn't.

In the half-shadow of the tree, Stevan lifted his head and gave them a look, then returned to his hunched posture.

"If he doesn't . . ." Emmi choked on the word.

"There are guards checking the roads now, and when day comes we'll comb the woods and fields," Heron said.

"Truly?" Emmi rubbed her forehead. "I don't remember."

"The Marchon's a parent, too, no matter that his children are grown."

"Was he here?" Emmi asked.

"No, Amara told him." Heron pulled away, leaving a cold void behind, only to return with a half-full mug. "She brought word when she stopped by."

Emmi drained the mug in small sips, frowning at the lukewarm spiced water. Then looked around for Amara.

"She went back to talk to the Marchon."

"He's having guards look for Su, not just the cat?" Emmi asked.

"Susa first and foremost." Heron grinned for a moment. "The cat can probably look after himself."

"If only there were more . . . more to do." Emmi clutched the mug tight, knuckles turning gray. "If you could Dance her back."

"We're trying—Stevan's trying"—Heron sighed—"but there are limits to compeer magic."

"Limits?"

Gisela rolled over and sat up, shifting closer to Emmi and Heron. Voice low, she said, "He's doing his best, but he's never met Susa and there are a lot of people here, in the camp and the city, and a lot of traffic along the roads. He has to tease out any signs of her."

"Wouldn't Dancing help?" Emmi didn't understand compeers, no matter that she'd seen them pairing with princesses. So many were taught, not born, and no one ever talked about what their magic was. Princesses, now, everyone knew the kinds of things they could do.

"Dance isn't . . . it's separate from what born compeers do," Gisela said. "Their magic makes them the best partners for princesses, but it's a different kind of thing."

"But when you Dance storms you sweep people out of floods, or you soothe the earth to avoid quakes as you did at Gisela's home,"—Emmi jerked her head, though she had no notion which direction Foleilion lay—"or make storms dump snow around cities rather than burying them as happens every winter at Tharis."

"That takes all thirteen of us in turns, at the Terparchon's direction." Heron shook their head, but the movement caused light to flare and reflect from their eyes suggesting they took Emmi's words to heart.

"If all of you do such big things, can't you Dance and find one little girl?" Emmi asked.

"We Dance underground," Heron said, voice blank of expression.

"You were out under the sky at that village," Emmi waved a hand in the same direction.

"Foleilion," Gisela said. A thoughtful note entered her voice, unless it was only Emmi's desperate hope hearing it. "It's true there are smaller things we can Dance, in ones and twos and threes."

"There were all those rumors before we left Yaris that Danissa Danced her father to health," Emmi shrugged off the top layer of cloth, a new warmth surging through her.

"True enough," Gisela said.

"Then can't you . . ." Emmi glanced back and forth between them. "Both of you, one of you?"

"I'm not sure where to begin." Gisela frowned. "I've never started a solo Dance knowing what I was doing. I haven't even been a princess a year."

"It's true princesses in other lands sometimes Dance smaller things. The princess in Kitiva used to Dance for rain, or more often for it to stop raining, though I never knew how much magic they or their Dances had." Heron stood and drew in a long breath, then looked down to meet Emmi's gaze. "I'll try, not just for you, but for Susa who's no doubt missing you."

18

Heron paced the edge of the area in front of Emmi's tent to get an idea of how much room they'd have to move about. The earth was hard-packed and dusty after so many folk tromping through in the wake of Susa's disappearance. Tents packed together more tightly than around the princesses and compeers—but the main difference lay in the matter of open space. The princesses and compeers' tents all faced a central, shared common space with wide avenues at three points that led to the cook tents, city, and nearest privy area.

In contrast, whoever had laid out this section of tents had pitched them so that each had a small space in front outlined by the backs of other tents, none far from wide avenues that stretched between cooks and privies.

Heron had less space than if they Danced before their own tent—three medium steps covered any side—but more privacy.

How much would it matter? Likely not at all. The problem wasn't space but figuring out how to Dance finding a child. They pulled back memories of Dance after Dance that they'd done at the Terparchon's orders, or Amara's, all of which they'd written up for Stork. None seemed to fit.

Perhaps they could take the most recent Dance, in Foleilion, as inspiration. Outside, with the shifting breezes twining around them, Amara had led the princesses through locating faults in the earth nearby and easing the tension.

Of all things, that brought back memories of watching the princess in Kitiva at equinox festivals. Heron brushed a finger along the memory keeper resting over their heart. A strange connection to make, since there'd been six princesses in Foleilion while Kitiva rarely hosted more than one and then only when the current was training her— invariably *her*—successor. She'd made circular rounds, stooping to dig her hands into baskets set at regular intervals and gathering flower petals or leaves depending on the season, snowflakes in particularly rough years, to toss into the crowd.

Had the Kitivan princess even had princess magic? Heron had paid the matter little attention at the time—they hadn't sprouted princess magic until well into their fourth decade—but had the vague notion the princess chose her heir for grace and agility, and familial connections.

Perhaps something combining the two would work: seeking Susa instead of faults, and trying to summon her back rather than tossing out petals or leaves.

"I can try if you'd prefer," Gisela said as Heron completed a fifth round.

"How well do you know Su?" Heron stopped, glancing at Emmi huddling by the tent.

Gisela frowned and shrugged. "Well, you'll need a compeer. Do you want me to ask Zora?"

Even as she spoke, she grimaced.

Heron did likewise. "Only if necessary."

"Would you rather Stevan?"

Both glanced at the compeer seated against the tree, head in his hands.

"He needs to focus on finding Su, so no." Much as Heron would prefer working with Stevan, they lacked sufficient confidence to risk pulling him away from his task. "It's a small Dance, and small space. I'll try on my own."

After all, that's what the princesses in Kitiva did: Dance on their own more often than not. If they even Danced instead of danced. Heron didn't truly want compeer magic, but they did envy that born compeers had it from the start and never lost it, while princess magic came and went without warning or anyone knowing why or how.

"Is a compeer important?" Emmi asked.

"It helps," Gisela said. "We, princesses"—she gestured at Heron and herself —"can get lost in Dancing and not realize that we're stretching too far or leaning over so much we might lose balance. Compeers help keep us from falling or tripping or running into each other."

"Keep Heron from falling or tripping?" The blanket slipped from Emmi's shoulders as she rose, chin high although she shivered in the chill air. "I'll try."

Heron had been trying to not pay attention to their talk , but couldn't miss that. They turned, to find her steady on her feet but with a grayish cast under her skin.

"Are you sure?" Gisela asked.

"Yes." Emmi's chin rose higher. Her hands fisted at her side, but she bit her lip and tears lurked in the corners of her eyes.

"Very well," Heron said, then turned to catch doubt on Gisela's face. "Doing something will be good, and it might be easier for me to draw on the connection between Emmi and Susa."

Gisela shook her head, but moved back to make room.

"What do you need me to do?" Emmi took a step closer to Heron, only a hand's breadth of space between them. She had to tilt her head back to look up at them.

"Watch where I move. If it looks as though I'll bump into something, try to turn me away from it. If I tilt too far, brace me or ease me down." Heron reached to stroke her cheek, then pulled back. "But don't hurt yourself."

"Do you want a beat?" Gisela asked.

"May I?" Heron turned to Emmi.

A puzzled look covered her face, but she nodded.

Moving slowly, Heron laid a hand on her chest and searched for her pulse. She was warm to the touch, trembling slightly, and the rhythm of her heart speeding as they touched.

Heron patted their thigh to match, not stopping or pulling away until Gisela and an awakened Lysia had picked up the beat. Even Stevan, head still in hands, tapped his toes to it.

After a moment's indulgence, Heron let go of Emmi. Their fingers cooled quickly once away from her. They traced a small circle around the opening, moving to the beat. Planted feet firm on the ground, no matter the gouts of dust that rose and sparkled green in the light as they extended their hands. Fingers felt, then closed as though wrapping gently around small wrists, and pulled back.

A hint of magic trickled along their forearms and up their calves, but failed to make it past their elbows or knees.

The second round they took faster, two steps to each beat.

Third speeding up further. A sharp pang racked their arms, as though something grabbed *them* and dug deep. They overbalanced. Body stiff and straight, they nearly fell face-down—but Emmi was there, hands firm as she grabbed their shoulders and pushed them back upright.

Shock and warmth rippled through Heron—not at the near miss, but the contact. For the first time, they understood why the Terparchon allowed princesses to Dance with beloved partners as compeers when the partners were willing. Zora was a competent compeer, always present and ready to brace and catch Heron when they Danced—but Emmi made up for lack of dance knowledge with a solidity and trust and care for Heron despite her worry over Susa.

That one moment made Heron long to Dance with her under better circumstances—all the more when they realized the brief contact had an echoing spark in the distance. They couldn't tell quite where.

They tore away from Emmi's hands, loath though they were to lose the connection, and whirled in search of the spark. They lost the beat. Awareness of their surroundings dwindled likewise, as they followed the urge of their body and magic.

Finding Susa and bringing her home safe was the most important thing.

Where, where, where?

The air flared with magic. They stopped whirling and nearly fell again, but Emmi was there.

This time, before Heron could leap back into motion, a call shook them from their reverie.

"Meow!"

A cat stalked into the circle and glared at them. Smaller than Homer, with a coat of mixed gray and orange, it sat facing Heron and Emmi.

Another cat arrived with a quieter meow, then a third, fourth, and on until seven cats formed a line behind the first.

Gisela and Lysia faltered, their hands falling to their sides as they pulled back against the tents edging the area. Even Stevan stopped tapping the beat and lifted his head.

The cats stalked Heron and Emmi, pushing them back against Emmi's tent.

Seven took up positions forming a circle, facing inward and their eyes glowing green that owed little to the moss baskets.

The gray and orange cat remained in the center. It turned in a circle, tail flicking at each of the seven. The outer cats began to meow in chorus, their beat very similar to the one Heron had set earlier save perhaps a hair faster.

The central cat Danced. It rose up on its hind legs, paws, batting— at nothing Heron could see—then dropped and patted the still-invisible and perhaps non-existent thing around the circle. Again it rose, again fell, again played with something unseen.

Then it leapt, twisting as its limbs stretched wide. A second and a third, with such grace and dexterity as Heron had never seen among the princesses.

An urge to do their best to imitate, no matter how poorly, thrummed up from their soles.

The cat paused, raised up on its hind legs and turned glowing eyes on Heron. A paw summoned them.

They answered. Emmi's hands fell away as Heron entered the circle. The air warmed, tasting of earth with a hint of cat hair coating

Heron's tongue. They swallowed and Danced, playing with the cat and tossing imaginary treats for it to play with.

But all the while, Heron kept to the perimeter, stepping only a toe's length away from the encircling cats. The Dancing cat took the rest of the space, darting and playing.

Until all stopped. The meowing, Heron back where they'd started.

The Dancing cat stood at the very center. It yowled and leaped high, arching across the intervening space to land in Heron's quickly extended arms. Smaller and lighter than they'd expected, it touched noses with them before slipping through their fingers to sit at their feet staring inward.

As did Heron.

For a dome appeared where the cat had Danced. Lights flickered within, forming an image of a different space.

Susa curled in a blanket at the base of a tree. Homer lay next to her, eyes glowing with the same light as the other cats, and silver shining from their tail and face markings.

A third form sat on the far side of Homer, petting the cat: Alvi with a blanket around their shoulders. They leaned back against the tree. Their head whipped around and they blinked and frowned, but didn't seem to see Heron, Emmi, or the other humans and cats watching.

Emmi jerked, tilting forward and pushing past Heron—but too late.

"Meow!" The lead cat flicked their tail into the dome, and the image vanished. The cat's tail glowed. It stalked over to Stevan and whipped the tip against Stevan's nose.

"Found her." Stevan jumped to his feet, nearly overbalancing, but Gisela was there.

"Ohhh!" Emmi turned and buried her face against Heron's chest.

They held her as the cats stalked away. Rocked her as Stevan and Gisela raced off to report Susa's location.

Cradled her through the night as she alternately slept and waited for morning and her daughter's return.

19

Emmi had plenty of company when she waited by the roadside the next day. Heron stood behind her, helping keep the hordes back. So many crowding around, all talking at once making it hard to hear oneself think, not to mention the smell and feel of them pressing close. One and all in a clump along the edge of camp, leaving empty and in plain view the narrow track leading to the woods. Someone was selling cheese on a stick and doing brisk business.

Across the way, Zora drummed her fingers against her shoulders as she waited, with her father by her side.

Despite the warmth, Emmi shivered. She'd donned a clean blue tunic, but already the sides wrinkled under the clench of her fingers. Grains of sand in the corners of her eyes made them ache after the unsettled night.

Heron had been so caring, so kind—and glorious in Dance.

She'd actually slept some after, believing her daughter watched over by cat and human. Not merely a cat, but the same cat that despised Emmi—and cared for Susa.

Yet Emmi's surety had shriveled under the sun and the long wait from sunrise.

What if the Dancing cats were wrong? Or Susa and Homer had moved on? Or . . .

"Patience, they'll be here," Heron said.

She barely took in the words over the crowd, but couldn't begrudge their presence. They'd helped search for Susa and deserved to see her daughter's return.

Indeed, a hush fell when two guards emerged from the woods, their red and gold uniform tunics bright against the foliage.

Stevan and Alvi followed, and between them Susa. The girl's head was high, even at this distance, as she carried Homer.

Little registered except Susa. The scrapes along her arms and legs, the scratch on one cheek and bits of leaves stuck in her hair. The rents in her tunic, which was covered in cat hairs. The way her chin wobbled as she bent to let Homer down before turning to Emmi.

Everything else became a blur of cheers and smiles, pats and hugs from other children and Lysia and other children's attendants with permission.

And of holding Susa and never letting go.

Emmi wasn't sure how she and Susa managed to get back to their tent site alone. Perhaps Heron had helped, or the Marchon.

Or the lure of the market opening in the city, perhaps, since the area seemed quieter than usual. No stray thuds or grunts, or the smell of the next tent over where the family regularly forgot to wash dishes after meals.

Only Emmi and Susa in the rectangular expanse where Heron and cats had so recently Danced. Everything tidy, clothes in neat piles and a pitcher of water warming in the sun. The spices perfumed the air.

And Susa in Emmi's arms. Her daughter, real and warm and living and hugging her back.

Then squirming.

Emmi tightened her hold for one last minute, then let go. She sat back, in much the same spot she'd occupied the night before.

Her daughter remained close. The scratch on her face appeared minor, already scabbed over. Susa pouted, and her elbows pressed tight against her sides—but her right hand rubbed at the marks on her left arm while her left hand held tight to the hem of Emmi's tunic.

Losing Susa and not knowing where she was had been the worst Emmi had ever known. Figuring out what to say to the girl now that she was safe came nowhere near.

Still, Emmi's belly roiled and she swallowed trying to dispel the bitter tang of bile in her mouth.

An odd-shaped lump of cloth lay nearby, the deep brown fabric recognizable as one of Susa's oldest tunics only after several glances.

A tunic that Susa had taken with her.

How the bag had arrived there, Emmi wasn't sure. She hadn't brought it, or Susa. Perhaps Heron or Stevan—it didn't matter.

But it was a place to start. "Is that yours?" she asked. "What did you take with you?"

"Things." Susa shrugged.

"Clothes? Food?"

"Maybe." The girl's chin sank toward her chest.

"Enough to get you to Yaras?" Emmi asked.

"Maybe." Susa's head hung so low only the mass of curls and twigs and leaves at the top showed.

"You need a wash, and clean tunic, and food, and probably sleep." Emmi brushed a hand over the curls. The loosest of the leaves fell in pieces to the packed earth by Susa's feet. "We will talk about your going now or later, your choice, but there's no escaping. I'm so happy to have you back safe"—Emmi leaned in for a quick hug—"and so angry at you for going without . . . why?"

She bit her lip. All her fine talk about letting Susa adjust to being back, and the benefits of being back, then she had to go and risk it.

"I wanted to stay with uncle-aunt. I told you over and over." Susa picked at her messy hair, gaze still downcast.

"But then you were happy to come."

"Heron told me stories about all the neat things we might see, but we haven't seen anything we haven't ever before, and then they were" —Susa's head came up and she pointed at Emmi—"you were . . ."

"Kissing." Emmi nodded, tucking her hands in her lap to keep her fingers from twitching. Best to stay as calm as possible and hide how she trembled and feared to put a foot wrong. "It's something people do when they're older and they find someone they like."

"So you like them?"

"I thought you did too," Emmi said.

"I do, but . . ." Susa shrugged again, going back to picking at the twigs in her hair.

"They like you, just different from how they like me."

"Is this one of those things I have to be bigger to understand?" Susa started to stick out her tongue, then thought better of it.

"Yes." Emmi reached out slowly and drew Susa to lean against her. The girl hardly resisted, even rubbed her head against Emmi's shoulder. "Do you mind about me and Heron?"

"I guess not." Susa gave a big yawn.

"If you're tired of traveling, well, if your father's willing you could stay with him in Tharis all next year." Emmi made the offer, glad Susa couldn't see her face. The words hurt to say.

"But I want to see uncle-aunt!" Susa pulled back, eyes wide and mouth agape.

"Then you'll have to travel with me."

"Why can't I stay with him?" Another yawn and the whine in Susa's voice suggested a bath might have to wait until after a nap.

"Because you're my daughter, not Aurel's, and I love you, and I say so." Not to mention, Emmi could imagine Aurel's shock at the notion of having to watch out for Susa for nine months out of the year. "You don't have to decide about traveling with me and the court or staying with your father yet."

Susa gave a wordless murmur, wriggling against her mother.

"But you do owe thanks to everyone who got up in the dark to look for you," Emmi said.

"Everyone?" Susa asked.

"Everyone." Except the cats, but that was a topic best left for another time. "That includes Alvi for making them escort you here and go out of their way."

"But they were coming here!"

"Even so," Emmi said.

Susa grumbled, but she buried her head against Emmi's side to the point the words were lost to Emmi's tunic and Emmi knew her daughter spoke mostly because her face moved.

"And you owe Heron an apology and thank you, too." Emmi stroked her daughter's head. "They Danced for you, you know, to see where you were and make sure you were all right."

She waited as the girl remained still—and was rewarded after a few minutes when Susa nodded against Emmi's chest and turned her head far enough to say clearly "Heron, too."

Emmi sighed. They'd have to talk this over more—Susa was spared a scold for now, but sooner or later needed to understand how much danger she'd run toward—but the way she said Heron's voice suggested the girl didn't resent them. She'd run away, but toward her uncle-aunt rather than to make her mother chose between her and Heron.

❦ 20 ❧

People of all description thronged the market. Elbows and shoulders brushed Heron's arms and back. A late-arriving merchant in a travel-stained tunic and mantle pushed through followed by a servant in tunic only, carrying a box redolent of sonnewood likely used to keep away insects and almost overriding the sweaty aroma clinging to them.

A small child rode high atop their parent's shoulders, arms flinging wildly and fingers briefly catching in Heron's hair. The parent muttered an apology before the crowd carried them away.

So many groups of two, three, and more. Although certain others ventured to the market alone, Heron's gaze kept catching on those who clearly belonged together.

Friends. Lovers. Families.

Merchant booths lined either side of the wide expanse, each ablaze with color and motion. Brightly painted signs proclaimed spices available for purchase here, impossible to scent through the welter of sweat and perfume. Lengths of cloth draped the top of a wagon across the way, drawing those interested in fine fabrics.

A family of three circled around Heron, each carrying sticks that pierced through layers of pickled vegetables in greens, purples, and reds.

Heron turned to mark where they'd purchased the treat, something *they* would happily buy—if only they had someone to share with. Their simple orange tunic and light mantle in matching colors had already picked up grease marks from someone's passing.

Nothing about them indicated their rank. Most of the other princesses and compeers likewise had foregone their gilded and silvered cords or circlets. Gisela and Stevan bargained with a ribbon merchant several lengths down. Zora stalked through the center of the street. People made way for *her* as they didn't for Heron, even though a guard attending her followed discreetly behind rather than before.

Heron had a guard shadow as well, but one who lingered far enough back to allow them the illusion of being on their own.

Illusion? Reality. The guard watched to ensure they remained safe and unharmed in body and magic, not in heart.

Still, none of the crowd brushing by had touched the small coin purse tucked under Heron's belt—or the thin, much-folded square of parchment nestled next to it.

They wended through the throng, pausing here and there—the silks on offer at one cloth merchant were lovely and soft to the touch —before winding up at Stork's cart.

The wooden doors at the back of the cart were thrown open and covered with a layer of dark-blue velvet that swayed as the crowd eddied. Trinkets pinned against the cloth glittered: a wooden comb enameled with red flowers, a jointed doll dressed in a yellow robe, a heavily embroidered memory keeper, and more.

Two long, thin drawers overflowing with goods for sale rested atop wooden frames sturdy despite being collapsible. Heron didn't miss the painstaking labor required to set them up, still remembered from the one time they'd traveled with their uncle.

Stork stood behind the drawers, forehead damp and teeth flashing as they bargained over a carved, scented comb. Eager buyers crowded near, turning over the combs and toys—but few hands touched the half-dozen memory keepers at the far end.

Heron brushed their chest, where their memory keeper rested beneath their tunic.

Three children dashed through the crowd, feet thudding against the hard earth despite their small size. The frame and drawer swayed slightly, just enough to make the spray of stars embroidered on one memory keeper sparkle. Heron picked it up and turned it over.

The stars were neatly laid in silver thread flush with the dark-green background. Very well made, though the top stuck for a moment. It flipped open, hinged at the end rather than being a separate piece. The inside smelled of nothing and yet brought home—Kitiva—to mind.

Shivering, Heron slipped the parchment from their belt and kept it pressed against their palm. They waited until Stork glanced their way, then tucked the paper inside and restored the top. Brushing hands across the memory keepers, they left it with the others piled atop.

Stork nodded as Heron left.

Heron let the crowd carry them past three more carts—another trinket merchant, one selling cloth, and the source of the pickled veggies. The crowd seethed around them, pushing them toward the edge, as the Marchon and members of the city council paused to speak with vendors on the far side.

Finding a vendor offering cool drinks, they handed over a small coin embossed with the Terparchon's profile. The merchant's young assistant dipped a ladle into a barrel of pink liquid with motes of ice floating atop. Overly sweet, it coated Heron's mouth and they had to fight to keep their expression even as they declined a second sip.

Instead, they forged their way to a fountain at the far end. A cat in a majestic pose despite the greenish cast to the metal sat atop an equally green-tinged fish twice its size. Water trickled from the broad fish mouth into a broad, low-lipped basin.

Heron nodded at the trio of living cats drinking. One lifted its head and meowed, flicking its tail much as it had before. With a nod to Heron, it stalked off followed by the others.

Surely a person might drink where a cat did. Heron filled cupped hands and cleaned their mouth.

"Enjoying the market?" Alvi appeared nearby, waiting their turn to wash hands and drink.

"Well enough." Heron stepped back and nodded. "I haven't seen you yet since this morning to thank you for your care of Susa."

"No need," Alvi said. "I've already been thanked by Emmi and Susa, and half the other people here, though they can't all have been witness. Speaking of Emmi and Susa, I think they're looking for you."

Fewer people were near, most lingering close to the booths that started several arm's lengths away. Even Heron's shadow guard stuck to the edge of the crowd, leaving Heron ample room to breathe. The open space combined with Heron's height to allow them a good vantage to search the crowd, but fruitlessly. Emmi and Susa were short enough to hide within the crowd whether or not they wanted to.

"I'll find them, or they me." Heron shrugged. "Have you left your village for good?"

"For now." Alvi shifted, putting the fountain between them and the trading area. "This is more strangers than I've ever seen at one time before, but I'll have to adjust. I know what I'm looking for even if I don't know how I'll find it."

"You might see if you can travel with a trader, someone who knows ways to get about," Heron said. "Some of the smaller traders enjoy company."

"That's a fine idea." Alvi opened their mouth to say more, then grinned and moved away.

Heron turned to find Emmi and Susa heading right for them. Both wore good tunics in deep shades of green that almost concealed the creases attesting that the cloth had been tucked away in a trunk.

Emmi marched forward, one hand clasped with her daughter who dragged behind.

Heron's lips twitched as they tried to smile. The muscles in their legs and arms jerked until they locked their knees and pressed their arms tight against their sides.

Susa jerked free of Emmi and lurched forward to wrap her arms around Heron's waist. "I'm sorry," she muttered over and over against their belly, words muffled and felt as much as heard.

Emmi stopped an arm's length away and coughed.

Susa let go and stepped back against her mother, head down.

Heron dropped to their knees, heedless of the dust staining their tunic, and held out a hand. "I'm glad you're okay."

"Are you mad at me?" Susa asked.

"I was worried, but your mother was frantic," Heron said.

Emmi coughed, an odd sound, but Heron didn't dare glance her way. They focused on the young girl instead.

"Are we still friends?" they asked.

"Hand-holding friends." Susa nodded, then grimaced and glanced at her mother. "But not kissing friends."

"Not you and me, no. But I'd like to be kissing friends with your mother." Heron remained on their knees, waiting through the long silence that all the rumble of the crowd couldn't break.

Susa shrugged, scuffing a sandaled foot against the earth. "I guess that's all right. If *she* likes it."

"I'll take that," Emmi said.

"So will I." Heron rose and met her gaze, but didn't kiss her despite Susa's grudging permission.

They wanted their next kiss somewhere more private.

Susa started back through the market with one hand in Heron's grasp and the other holding tight to her mother. She let go soon enough as she looked over all the treasures on offer.

Heron reached for their purse once, but after the pointed glare from Emmi they kept their funds to themselves. Though they took note of what Susa liked—and Emmi—for possible later purchase.

Despite not getting any new toys from Heron or Emmi no matter how Susa pleaded—though she did win a sip of the cold pink liquid, which she seemed to like much better than Heron—the child became more and more at ease with both of them. Every time she darted over to glance at a merchant's offerings, Heron drifted close enough to Emmi to hold hands. Sometimes Susa pushed between them after, but others she'd hang on the other side of her mother or Heron.

Warmth and hope flowed in Heron's veins as they remained behind while Emmi took a starting-to-be-fretful Susa back to camp to rest. The gentle sway of Emmi's hips raised the heat in Heron's blood, while the sweet smile on her face the few times she glanced back fed the hope.

"You care for them." Stork nudged Heron with a shoulder. He took a bite out of the red pepper at the top of a full stake of pickled veggies. No doubt he'd swapped with a neighboring trader to watch while he wandered and ate.

"Yes," Heron said.

"Will you bring them when you come back to Kitiva?" Stork didn't turn to face Heron—or Heron to him—until Emmi and Susa vanished through the city walls.

"If I come back to visit I would certainly hope so." Heron shook their head when Stork offered the stick to them. "I doubt Emmi will let Susa go far from her anytime soon."

"I heard about the commotion, but . . . visit? Not stay?" Stork asked.

"I may stay here."

"Because they understand you"—Stork waved the stick at the crowds behind them—"and we don't."

"Codarans accept me as I am." Heron studied their uncle, unsure where the new, strange note in his voice came from. Perhaps he'd appreciated the latest missive. A quick glance confirmed that their shadow guard lurked several paces away, but they dropped their voice all the same. "You've found the paper I left you?"

"What?" Stork asked.

"A description of the Dances I've been part of since the last one I gave you. I wrote about the cats Dancing with me last night, and that gave me some idea about ways to defend through Dance." Heron rubbed their hands. "I don't have them worked out yet, but in a moon or so, but come see me in Tharis and I'll have some suggestions.

"What paper?"

"I slipped it into the memory keeper. You saw me do it. You nodded." Heron shrugged. "It should be safe enough. You never seem to sell them."

"Almost never." Stork wiped their forehead, skin taking on a greenish cast. "I didn't realize and I sold one today, the green with silver stars."

"Before you took out the paper?" Heron asked, a sinking sensation in their belly.

"Exactly, so now you'll have to get it and give it to me later."

"Who did you sell it to?"

Stork pointed at the gate through which Emmi and Susa had left. "The woman you're sweet on."

❧ 21 ☙

Emmi cradled the memory keeper in her hands as she sat in front of her tent. The tiny stitches formed a sleek whole that warmed the longer she held it.

Long shadows crossed her lap, the clearing, and the tent, as the sun sank low in the sky. Savory smells wafted from the upwind market. Although Emmi hadn't eaten much over the day, she wasn't hungry—or not enough to leave her place.

Soft snoring assured her that her daughter slept, that she hadn't slipped out and run off again. The girl had made it through much of the day, and all of the most important apologies, before dropping. Emmi had only to stretch a hand out to her side and slightly behind to touch Susa's hand, and let the soft skin offer more reassurance.

They had the camp largely to themselves. Most of their neighbors were off enjoying the market. The next night there would be a banquet with the Marchon hosting the city council and leading merchants, and surely some of the cooks devoted time to preparations, as Aurel had on the two occasions he'd followed the progress. This night, however, folk mingled.

Zora had been kind enough to give Emmi the whole day to spend with Susa. *"I can care for myself when needed,"* she'd said, cuddling and cooing over her cat, who'd glared at Emmi.

For all that Homer had accompanied Susa on her adventure, Emmi felt no greater fondness for him.

The other cats, those who'd Danced with Heron to find Susa, had a place in Emmi's heart.

They'd helped. Then again, so had Emmi. The merest memory of the night made Emmi's fingers tingle with the energy that had flowed through her.

One of the strangest and most beautiful things she'd experienced in her life. She'd followed Heron as they swayed back and forth. Stretched out her hands to brace them as they bent over. The ground had seemed extra firm beneath her, as though her feet had grown roots descending deep. No matter how much of Heron's weight rested against her, she kept them on their feet. It was all so very different from watching them Dance, or holding them, even kissing them, yet also strangely intimate.

"Meow?"

Emmi jerked, body stiffening.

A cat pawed at Emmi's hands, claws hidden and pads soft. It wasn't Homer but the gray-orange one who'd Danced the night before.

"Meow." The cat rose, stretching as it had the night before, and batted at the memory keeper with both front paws.

"You want this?" Emmi asked.

"Meow." The cat sat, head tilted to one side.

Emmi's fingers tightened around it. She hadn't known what she was looking for until she'd found it earlier in the day.

While wandering the market with Susa, Emmi had paused by a cart offering Kitivan goods for sale. The merchant's soft accent had caught Emmi's attention, as he bargained with a father over a jointed wooden doll. Then Susa paused, caught by the toys, but Emmi had chosen to linger, too. The merchant's voice was so similar to Heron's, and their faces so resembled each other that she couldn't help but wonder if they were related.

Her fingers stroked over the goods, tempted by nothing until she spotted the row of long, thin tubes at the back. She'd seen Heron wearing something similar, and they'd mentioned it holding memories of people and places they loved.

Maybe that would make a good gift, for when she was ready to give them one. Something to hold new memories they could make together.

Susa pulled at Emmi and pointed at a trader marching down the street with racks of sweets, trailed by several children and parents. She stopped when the merchant stooped and grinned at her.

"Welcome to a little corner of Kitiva." The merchant glanced back and forth between Emmi and Susa. "I am Stork and would be happy to assist you in selecting a suitable treasure."

"You look like Heron." Susa winced when Emmi grabbed her hand.

She'd thought the same thing, but . . . "What do we say when people introduce themselves?"

"Nice to meet you." Susa kicked at the packed ground.

"No offense taken." Stork nodded at Emmi, then turned back to her daughter. "It's only right I look like him, or rather him like me, for he's my nephew."

"Who?" Susa's face scrunched in puzzlement.

"Heron, he's my nephew."

"But Heron's not a *he*." Susa rolled her eyes. "Everybody *always* says it's polite to call people how they want to be called."

Emmi's face flared with heat. Amusement rippled through her, but she knelt next to Susa, squeezing the girl's shoulder. "Is there anything else we always say?"

Susa frowned, evidently trying to think it through as the merchant gave a half-laugh that faded and left them jiggly.

Emmi leaned in and whispered in her daughter's ear, lips brushing soft strands of hair. "Be nice." Then she stood and smiled at the merchant. "I was looking for something for Heron, as it happens, and I noticed the memory keepers. Do people—Kitivans—ever wear more than one?"

"Oh, oh, yes, the older one gets the more keepers one needs." Stork straightened and snatched up the thin tubes and laid them out before Emmi. "Heron was just looking at them. He—er they"—Stork glanced down at Susa—"liked this."

Susa watched Emmi bargaining, arms crossed over her chest. Emmi had to hide bemusement at how this disconcerted the merchant to the point he let it go for a good price.

The instant they turned away, before they took so much as a step and got lost in the crowd and noise, Susa grabbed her mother's hand and yanked. "Be nice means I wasn't supposed to correct him? But he was wrong!"

"Even so." Emmi tucked the memory keeper into her belt.

"So many rules. Do I have to apologize to *him* too?" the girl asked.

Emmi glanced back and caught a look of horror on Stork's face.

"Not this time," she said as she hurried her daughter away.

"Meow!"

A claw lightly scratched against Emmi's hand brought her back to the present. A thin white line marred her palm, but the cat hadn't drawn blood.

The creature pawed again at the hand holding the memory keeper, tail lashing.

Emmi held it out.

The cat sniffed at the end and sneezed. Then it sprawled across the ground and groomed furiously. A cloud of gray and orange hairs floated in the air then fell in a semi-circle around it. Ceasing the furious pawing at its head and body, it patted the hairs into a small pile in front of Emmi. One paw brushed the top of the pile, then the memory keeper.

"You want me to put some in?" Emmi asked.

"Meow."

Emmi struggled to open the top. It refused to unscrew, until finally she realized it flipped instead. She tried to whisk the cat hair inside, but there wasn't room. Her fingers brushed something soft and crinkly instead. Angling it to catch the fading sunlight, she discovered a thin roll of paper inside.

"Meow!" The cat batted at the memory keeper.

Pulling out the paper, Emmi set it aside. It rolled, but only as far as the edge of the tent. Scooping up a handful of soft cat hair, she stuffed it into the keeper.

Her reward was a purr and the cat rubbing against her. Maybe cats weren't so bad after all.

Except, a moment later, Homer raced into the clearing. He stopped on the far side, back arching and hair standing straight up. His jaw gaped wide, emitting a whining hiss.

The other cat flicked its tail at him and rubbed against Emmi.

Homer glanced behind, then darted in a circle around Emmi and the gray and orange cat, into the tent.

"Wha?" Susa stopped snoring. "Hi, Homer."

Emmi turned to find her daughter sitting up and holding Homer close. The cat seemed to have shrunk in size, uttering faint, plaintive mews as it pressed against Susa.

The gray and orange cat moved to sit in front of tent, head up and body alert.

Emmi rose, swaying as faint tremors passed through the ground.

Zora thundered through the tents following Homer's path, but this wasn't the Zora Emmi usually dealt with. Not any Zora Emmi had even met before. She walked taller, straighter, and her feet hit the ground hard. The hem of her gilt-trimmed purple tunic snapped around her ankles and matching gilded sandals.

"Come back, you idiot!" Zora's lips curled in a snarl.

"Is there anything you need from me?" Emmi remained in front of the tent, the cat before her.

Zora braced, hands on hips, opposite. "Where is that cat?"

The gray and orange cat rose, back arching, and hissed at Zora.

"Not *you*." Zora waved at the cat, then her gaze shifted to Emmi. "The white and gray that hangs around all the time."

"Homer?" Emmi asked.

"Cats have nine lives, they don't need names." Zora lifted her chin. "You know the one I mean."

"Homer went by." Emmi mimicked Zora's gesture, waving in the general direction of the area behind the tent.

The gray and orange cat hissed again.

"I'll find it myself." Zora stomped toward Emmi, then turned at an angle and headed around the tent. She kicked the scroll and uttered her own hiss, then bent and scooped it up.

"Ah, that's mine." Emmi reached out, but didn't dare snatch it back. "It was in this when I bought it." She waved the memory keeper.

Zora gave Emmi no more than a quick sideways glance, busy taking in every inch of it.

Though whatever the compeer saw, Emmi missed. Instead of the usual characters spelling out words, it was covered in symbols. Stars, whirling circles, odd squiggles, mostly unfamiliar.

Emmi hovered close, but Zora gave her no chance to retrieve the paper as she rolled it back up. Head and chin high and gaze dark, face shadowed with the fall of evening, she turned to Emmi. "Where did you say you got this?"

"At the market."

"From whom?" Zora asked.

The gray and orange cat shifted to stand between Emmi and Zora. Glancing down at the cat, then into the tent, Emmi caught the glitter of Homer's eyes briefly before he ducked under Susa's bedroll. Susa curled around the lump of cloth and cat. Little though Emmi wanted to answer the questions, better that than draw Zora's attention to Homer and Susa.

"A vendor named Stork," Emmi said.

"Stork." Zora tapped the paper against her chin. "Kitivan?"

"Yes."

"Any relation to Heron?"

Emmi shivered, but the answer fell from her lips too readily. "He said Heron was his nephew?"

"That fits." Zora nodded. "If either comes looking for this"—she raised the paper high—"tell them to come to the Marchon's tent."

She stalked off, this time light as a feather—or a cat.

Susa crawled out from tent holding a shivering Homer. The gray and orange cat rubbed against Susa's legs and purred for a moment. Homer mewed back.

Emmi kept shivering. She longed to stay and comfort Susa, even if it also meant coddling Homer, yet Amara's voice echoed in her head telling her to come and tell Amara if Homer ran from Zora. Worse, had Emmi just gotten Heron in trouble? Faced with a choice between speaking of Heron and protecting Susa, Emmi hadn't hesitated a moment.

The gray and orange cat meowed and flicked its tail at Emmi, then in the direction of the princesses and compeers' tents. A clear order.

Emmi should go find Amara to report Homer had run from Zora? Or seek out Heron?

❧ 2 2 ☙

Heron followed a twisty line between small encampments toward the tall, bright red and yellow tents of the Marchon and his immediate advisers. A guard marched ahead, their calf-length tunic a hair darker than the red of the tents. Another followed Heron, keeping time so closely with their forward counterpart as to match thuds as boots hit the ground. This remained true whether crossing hard-packed earth between tents or the slightly soggy rock-strewn dip where a meager creek trickled. The long knives hanging from their belts did not clack against their sides in unison, but that offered little consolation.

All was quiet around, save for the footsteps, knives, and the occasional call of birds overhead. Nearly everyone on the progress had gone into the city to enjoy the market. Perhaps some remained behind here and there, but none near enough to make noise. Even the bustle of the market seemed distant as though swallowed by the growing shadow of twilight.

No one around to see Heron marched and escorted by guards.

No witnesses.

No answers, either, only questions. Heron had been partway

through camp, heading for Emmi's site, when the guards spotted them and passed word that they were needed in the Marchon's tent.

Now.

Presumably needed by the Marchon, but for no reason that came readily to mind. If there were cause for a Dance, someone would ring the bells rather than send guards out in search of wandering princesses.

A few other guards, in similar uniforms and armed with knives or spears, stood in a five-star pattern around the Marchon's tent. Unlike most of the camp, it stood high enough Heron didn't have to dip their head as they passed through the opening. Poles at center and around the edge supported the weight of the bright canvas—and light baskets that made it glow outside and inside. A filmy curtain that fluttered with every movement concealed a third of the space, and the rest featured chairs arranged around a table with a few trunks at the edge in the shadows. Papers formed three messy piles atop the table, edges every which way.

All that space—but only two people stood within. The Marchon stood out no matter where he went, with a solid build and muscles that gave the impression he wore mail even when clad only in gold tunic and mantle. His cap of brown hair remained bright, little darker than his clothing. Wrinkles wreathed his eyes in pale lines almost invisible against skin the color of old parchment save when the shadows were right. His legs were paler than his face, bare toes almost invisible in the thick red rug covering the front half of the tent.

He remained still as Heron followed the guard in.

Zora, the other tent occupant, paced the inner sides of the rug. Her skirts whipped around her. Even the fringe edging her mantle rustled around her arms as she moved. Short and slight, she hardly resembled her father save hints in the shape of her head and the proportions of her hands. Fisted, she pressed them against her thighs with every step.

The sun had warmed the tent during the day, but cooler air wove around Heron's ankles as they entered, and they could practically measure the different temperatures from ground chill to warmth at the top. But that was no more than to be expected. Indeed, the impression was of a stolid father and upset daughter—hardly reason to summon Heron to join them.

"Thank you for coming," the Marchon said to Heron, then turned and nodded at the guards. "You may wait outside."

"Don't go far." Zora ceased pacing and waved a warning finger at them.

The Marchon turned to look at her, head only moving. She stared back for a long moment, the air fairly crackling between them until she dropped her gaze.

A muscle in Heron's back began to twitch. Zora was the compeer they'd partnered with numerous times over the years. She looked no different from any other time they'd seen her, yet the note in her voice sent shivers rippling through them.

"I appreciate your coming so promptly." The Marchon pulled the chairs away from the table and waved for Heron to take a seat if they liked. "I hope you were not summoned at an inconvenient time?" He sent another glance at his daughter.

"The guards were discreet. I was returning from the market when they asked me to come see you, but offered no information as to why. How may I be of service?" Heron remained standing, unwilling to sit when neither of the others did. It wasn't clear who summoned them, but they could guess why. A square of parchment rested at the near side of the table, showing marks of having been folded, rolled, and crumpled. Still, the symbols visible from a distance were familiar.

"Very prettily said." Zora grabbed the parchment and fanned it in front of Heron. Can you deny you wrote this?"

"I can't be certain without seeing it closer." Heron inclined their head but moved no nearer.

"Give it here." The Marchon held out a hand.

Zora clutched it close, but her father waited.

One breath, two, three.

She put it in his hand. Without word or sign of acknowledgment, he pivoted and returned it to the table. A wave of his hand offered—ordered—Heron to look it over.

Two steps were enough for Heron to recognize it—the symbols and the slightly wobbly way in which they'd been inscribed. The muscle in their back continued to twitch, but otherwise a slight feeling of relief coursed through them. It was the most recent missive they'd written for Stork, the one that had gone astray.

The Marchon also studied it, then looked over at Heron with a raised eyebrow. "I don't recognize all the symbols, but it seems to describe a Dance."

"See!" Zora marched to the far side of the table and rested her hands on it, leaning forward.

"Two Dances," Heron said.

"Indeed." Another wave of the Marchon's hand, this one an order to continue.

"Both were performed out in the open, where any might see. This is a summary of the Dance at Foleilion"—Heron pointed at the top of the parchment, then the lower—"and the smaller Dance I did the other night to help find Susa."

"You admit it!" Zora leaned even further in, looming over the parchment and shadowing the symbols.

"What have I done that anyone else who saw them could not do?" Heron asked. They didn't have the other descriptions given to Stork, or so Heron hoped. They swallowed, mouth dry, but remained straight and still. Cool air wrapped around them higher with every moment that passed, chilling the line of sweat along their spine.

"That does beg the question how many others saw both?" The Marchon rubbed his chin.

"Few, but there were some. And . . . there were cats at both Dances, and a cat Danced with me the other night. There are many cats at Kitiva, though I've never seen any show interest in Dancing." Heron shrugged. It seemed jerky to them but neither watcher blinked. "I thought it worth noting down."

"Dancing belongs to us." Zora snatched up the paper and pressed it against her midsection. "You cannot go sharing it with anyone."

"There are princesses in Kitiva, Sirasas, Orfelth, and near a half-dozen other cities I've visited." Heron stepped back, angling to face the Marchon without letting Zora out of sight. "Perhaps only a few, or no more than one at a time, unlike the dozen in Codaros, but princesses."

"Stealing our secrets." Zora's lips pulled back from her teeth.

"The Dances were done in the open," Heron repeated.

"Thief! Spy!"

"Enough." The Marchon snapped their fingers and pointed at the parchment. He stared at his daughter until she returned the paper to the table. His voice softened as he continued, "there is right on both your sides."

He opened his mouth to speak further, but heavy, hurried footsteps broke the thick, cooling air.

"Marchon?" a guard poked a head around the edge of the entry. "Amara's here and wants a word."

Even as her name was spoken, Amara swept in. She wore only a tunic, loose and old, though silvery sandals gleamed on her feet. Her white hair was pulled back in a thick braid down her back. She took one long glance around. Focusing on the Marchon, she extended both hands, palms up. "I believe I may speak to the matter at hand, if it is as I expect?"

"Of course, your counsel is always welcome." The Marchon nodded. "Compeer Zora has brought word of possible espionage: the conveyance of descriptions of Dances by Princess Heron to one not of Codaros."

Heron stiffened. There wasn't any sign of Stork anywhere—surely there'd be some sign if Heron's uncle were taken. Or had they chosen to talk to Heron first?

"Is the one not of Codaros a Kitivan?" Amara asked.

"Does it matter?" Zora crossed her arms over her chest, still looming over the table and the crumpled parchment.

"Most assuredly it does since Heron is involved." Amara shifted, facing Heron but with one hand still outstretched to the Marchon. "What did you write?"

A shiver racked Heron, but they'd already said as much so no reason not to repeat it. "Descriptions of the Dance at Foleilion and here, the other night." After she remained silent and raised an eyebrow, they continued—"and about the cats present at both, and Dancing with me here."

"Then I am glad to have come in time." Amara dusted her hands.

There is no crime and no wrong." She glanced around. Picking up the paper in question, she read over it and then rolled it back up. With a snap, she offered it to Heron.

"No!" Zora hurried around the table, seeming to grow taller as she pushed between Amara and Heron.

"The Terparchon knows," Amara said.

"But—"

"The Terparchon, the ruler of Codaros, is fully aware that Heron shares information about Dancing with Kitiva." Amara stared at Zora.

"What?" Heron clapped a hand over their mouth, only slightly relieved to realize the Marchon had said something similar at the same time.

Amara and Zora continued to stare at each other until Zora looked away.

With a nod for Heron, and the parchment offered again, Amara angled to face the Marchon. "When the Terparchon invited Heron to join the princesses, she accepted that they might share information about Dancing with their homeland."

"Did she now." The Marchon rubbed his chin, then shrugged.

Glancing at Heron, Amara asked, "what did you promise the Terparchon when she made the offer?"

"She told me the most important thing princesses did was help protect her land and people, and that"—the Terparchon's voice rang in Heron's memory even as they repeated her words—"she would never ask me to choose between homes and peoples, only to do what I could for the well-being of all."

"Interesting." The Marchon turned to his daughter. "In that case, there is no wrong here."

Zora shivered, head tilted down, and her voice very quiet and subdued. "I apologize—I didn't know . . . I hope you'll forgive me."

The shift unnerved Heron. They'd known Zora had several different selves, but never seen her shift from one to another so clearly.

With barely a glance Heron's way, Zora slipped from the tent.

The Marchon started after her, but stopped when Amara brushed his arm. Instead, he sank into a chair, rubbing his forehead.

Amara sighed and took a seat opposite him, glancing between him and Heron. "It probably would be best if Zora does not partner Heron in a Dance for a while. A princess needs to trust their compeer."

"She did what she thought best," Heron said. It wasn't the first thing that came to mind, or the third, but they didn't want to be seen leaping at a change in partners.

"Even so." The Marchon waved at Amara. "Who Dances with whom is your business. I'm a compeer, but only barely."

"You're more than you know, and I've Danced with you so I think my word is to be trusted on that point." Amara gave the Marchon a level look, then turned an impish smile on Heron. "It might be interesting to try partnering you with Emmi, if she's willing. She served as a compeer of sorts the other night, so perhaps you'll be so good as to ask her?"

"Emmi?" Heron tightened their leg muscles, trying not to shake too clearly. Waves of relief poured over them, along with mystification as to how Emmi came into the matter.

Then memory flooded through—Emmi had unknowingly walked off with the parchment from Stork's cart.

She's the one who came with news you might be in trouble," Amara said. "Whether or not you're willing to ask her to be your compeer, at least for a while, you should probably talk to her. She's likely imagining the worst."

Heron could easily imagine all manner of worse scenarios—themself taken and put to the question, their uncle, and anyone else they'd ever so much as sneezed at. Near drenched with sweat and relief, they bowed and took leave of the Marchon and Amara.

Taking Amara's advice, they started off in search of Emmi.

❦ 23 ❦

Heron's legs quivered with every step. Their lungs ached, breath coming in pants. They stumbled down to the edge of the creek and dropped onto a large boulder. Although rough and slanted, it offered a solid place to sit, think, and recover. Hands resting on their thighs, their fingers cold lines that twitched as tremors rippled through their body.

To one side, a line of light baskets formed a greenish line from the Marchon's camp to the rest of the tents. More glimmers in the distance limned the different segments of the camp across the fields. The princesses and compeers' section glowed to the right. Emmi's tent lay hidden among the mix of shadows and flares further behind.

Twisting bands of fog rose from the water trickling near Heron's feet, blending the separate lights and the growing gloom of twilight into a bewildering mix.

Or perhaps the misty scene was a mirage—Heron's sight reproducing their confusion and uncertainty.

They still belonged in Codaros. Amara and the Marchon had affirmed that, reiterating the Terparchon's initial offer—and the assurance that she'd understood Heron couldn't—wouldn't—leave Kitiva behind in becoming Codaran. The two leaders embodied why Heron had trod a painfully careful line in deciding what details to pass to Stork.

Yet the Marchon and Amara's encouragement failed to wash away the pain of Zora's anger and certainty of Heron's betrayal.

Zora! After Dancing with Heron time after time, letting them trust her to support and direct them. They'd partnered with other compeers, especially during their first confusing year, but increasingly had been assigned to Zora. For all their many differences, height being the most salient in Dance, they'd meshed well—or so Heron had always believed.

Dance required trust. Heron had seen flashes of anger in Zora on occasion. Then again, who didn't sometimes lose their temper when they came down wrong or misread signs and wound up crashing into each other.

Still, they'd relied on that assumption of underlying respect, only to have it torn away.

If Heron was so wrong about Zora, might they be equally wrong about Emmi?

Except, they hadn't been wrong to trust in the fair judgment of the Marchon, or for support and encouragement from Amara.

They were safe, for now. But what of their uncle? Should they face the crowds and head into the market to warn Stork? Yet that might put him in danger and make them appear more guilty. Suspicions and fears tumbled through them, internal echoes of the tremors still racking them.

"Meow!"

Heron started at the irritated demand, so close by.

A form stepped through the wreathing mist and shadow, resolving into Zora with Homer cradled in her arms. The cat's eyes glowed green as he meowed again, head butting against Zora's stroking hand.

Zora stopped several steps away. Homer's meow shifted to a purr. Gray cat hairs shone silver mixed with orange-gold across Zora's tunic and mantle, despite the fading light.

"I'm sorry," she said.

Heron drew in a deep breath, then rose to their feet. Safer to stand, though they remained in place rather than draw nearer. "You could have come and asked me, after all the times we've Danced together."

"*We've* Danced."

"How many are you then? For I've Danced with two or three of you." Heron lifted their chin and resisted the urge to snarl. This might be a different Zora than the one who'd denounced them, but the two shared a mind and body so how far apart could they truly be?

"You haven't Danced with *her*." Zora held the cat close, rubbing her chin against the top of Homer's head. "We, the rest of us, mostly me, don't let her be in control often. She's all anger and fear most of the time, though she doesn't try for control either. She sort of sits and seethes."

"She's not you, I understand that." Heron hadn't missed Zora skipping over their question as to how many she was. "But she also is, because I didn't know it was her I faced in the tent. I thought I knew the difference between your selves, but now I know that for a lie."

"I know it can't change anything, but I wanted to apologize this once. *We* did." The slight shift in Zora's voice suggested another self stepping forward.

It wasn't the same one Heron had faced in the Marchon's tent, at least they didn't think so, but the change unnerved them all the same. They swayed, muscles taut as they resisted the urge to step back—and instead nodded acknowledgment of the apology, if not acceptance.

Zora nodded back and turned to leave but paused and glanced around for a moment. "If you're looking for Emmi, she's at your tent."

The cat hairs adorning her continued to glow, marking her progress back up the incline toward the Marchon's tent.

Heron drew in a shaky breath, then crossed the narrow trickle of water. Their legs moved, feet steadier. Zora's apology, or the apology from one or two of those within Zora, helped a little, even if it didn't come from the seething anger that had accused Heron.

Bands of mist and fog lined the camp. Happiness and joy resounded in the distance as music and laughter blared over from the market on the far side of the city walls. Warm yellow light, bright in contrast to the muted light baskets, marked the celebrations.

Heron was glad most of the camp was having fun with the locals —

and gladder that it meant they were in the city and far away. The fewer who'd seen them marched through the camp the better, but also the fewer they saw now the better.

Guards making rounds constituted the few who remained to walk through the largely unpopulated encampment. They did so alone, which helped Heron breathe easier. Heron might tense when two guards approached them until memories faded and lost their sting.

As Zora had said, Heron found Emmi sitting cross-legged in front of their tent. Her tunic floated around her as she leaped to her feet. The low beams from the light baskets cast her face in sharp relief, making clear the upward curve of her lips and the way they trembled.

"Are you all right?" Emmi clasped her hands, waiting as Heron drew near. "I heard so many things."

"So will everyone else." Jumbled rumors always made circuitous paths around and through the court. No doubt they would be the subject of discussion and whispering and stares for days, weeks even, until some other surprise took over.

Heron dropped and sat near the side of their tent. Bending over, they buried their head in their hands. Yearning boiled through them to crawl into the tent and curl up in their bedroll, but they wanted as much or more to seek comfort from Emmi—if she was willing—and that ruled.

They jerked as Emmi wrapped a heavy mantle around their shoulders, not realizing how much they'd been shaking until the warmth penetrated and steadied them.

A few moments later, Emmi crouched in front with a mug of warm, spiced water.

The steam alone helped ease some of Heron's tension. They wrapped trembling fingers around the warm clay. Emmi shifted her hold to overlay theirs, supporting until they could hold it on their own.

The cup offered more warmth. The heated beverage infused strength.

Best of all, Heron took steadiness from Emmi's care. The more so because it wasn't her task anymore.

"I hope you don't mind me fussing over you. Fotis was here when I came. They'd have cared for you, but when I asked"—Emmi dropped to sit opposite Heron, but close enough for her breath to brush Heron's cheeks—"they offered instead to watch Susa."

"You don't mind being seen with me?" The question escaped them despite the obvious answer, given Emmi's presence and care.

"I worried you'd blame me." Emmi ducked her head.

"For what?" Heron took another sip, letting the warm liquid trickle down their throat and fuel their growing ease and hope.

"For letting Zora have the paper stuffed in the memory keeper." Her hand jerked toward her waist, and the movement allowed light to briefly reflect off the stars in the tube tucked under her belt. "Even after I realized you might have written it."

"You read it?"

"No." Emmi glanced away. "I didn't know any of the symbols."

Heron let out a deep breath. "It wasn't anything wrong, nothing the Terparchon didn't guess I might do." Though she'd never said outright and Heron had wondered at the last. "Ever since I became a princess here, I've sent descriptions of Dances back to Kitiva."

"Oh." Emmi stilled, face mostly hidden in shadow save when she moved into the slanted beam from a nearby basket. "You're a spy?"

"I hadn't thought of it that way, as I've never sent anything that couldn't be found some other way, but,"—Heron swallowed hard, raising the half-full mug to their lips—"whether or not I am a spy here, I have been a spy."

Better she know the whole of them now than learn later, even at the risk of her turning away.

"Have been?" she asked.

"I was a messenger for years and that's what most of us are. Spies." Heron breathed in the waning steam from the mug. "Even when we're just carrying messages and not tasked to find out secrets, we watch and listen and carry our impressions back."

"Did you ever dig for secrets?"

"Sometimes." More often than they liked to remember.

"In Codaros?"

Heron shrugged. They drank deep, letting the cooling water sit in their mouth as they slowly swallowed. When the silence continued, they sighed. "Maybe once or twice, but long ago. I hadn't been in

Codaros in years when I last came through and the Terparchon snatched me up for a princess."

"Long ago." Emmi echoed Heron's sigh, then shifted, eyes gleaming in the slanted light as she watched Heron. "Other than sharing Dances."

"Kitiva only has one princess at a time, a princess with an apprentice at best, and it's never been clear if the Kitivan princesses have magic. At least one princess in my lifetime died young without having chosen her successor." Heron set the empty cup down, fingers barely shaking. "So much knowledge has been lost that it seemed only fitting to share a little back."

"Would you ever go back and be their princess?" Emmi asked.

"No." Heron stiffened. "Maybe to visit, to teach or show, but I don't belong there anymore. I never fit even when I did belong, or thought I did. I want to stay here, as a Codaran."

They leaned forward, angling to catch the fullest view of Emmi's face. One hand rose to cup her cheek. "With you."

❧ 24 ❧

The weight of wanting rested heavy on Emmi's shoulders, along her back. Her hopes, theirs, both. The sharp angle of light from a basket illuminated the side of Heron's face, enough that their longing shone through. For her, certainly. Hard to doubt the soft, warm caress, the fingers brushing the side of her face. Yet longing for more than her—for being a Codaran and what that meant to them.

The distant rumble of music and laughter from the city made the quiet around them all the more immediate. They were alone. Folk might return at any time, but for these moments they had this part of the camp all to themselves. Anything disturbing the stillness came from Heron or her. Each sigh or indrawn breath—theirs.

Not even so much as a cat's footfall disturbed the stillness.

Nothing to distract her from Heron sitting before her with hope clear in their eyes—and their secrets laid bare for her knowing.

Over the years she'd served them, she'd seen them tired and worn yet without ever letting slip a hint of the complexities contained within. Despite their strained condition, they'd chosen to trust her.

Her.

Heron's fingers still curved along the line of her cheek. She wrapped a hand around them—her skin cool to their warm—and gently lifted away. Settling back on her haunches, she held on.

Her other hand fumbled at her belt. Throughout Heron's confession, Emmi had never once forgotten the stiff line of the memory keeper tucked at her side. It pressed hard enough to leave a bruise—but slipped out easy enough in the end.

Holding Heron's hand open, she laid the memory keeper on it. The stars twinkled in the light, the oblong length otherwise only slightly darker than Heron's skin.

"I bought this earlier because your uncle said you'd admired it."

A brittle laugh escaped Heron. Their hand shifted, stars twinkling the more with the movement. "He told me after. He hadn't realized what I'd done. My mistake, my haste . . ."

"Or just bad luck." Emmi pulled back, pressing her cold hands against her belly. "When I found the paper inside, I'd probably have taken it back to your uncle except Zora happened to pass by chance at that moment."

"Chance." Another bitter laugh, but at least Heron lifted it and turned it in the light to study the lines.

"She was chasing Homer." Emmi shivered at the memory, then forged forward. "But I found it, the paper, because I was putting something inside."

Heron drew a sharp breath in, arms clasping against their side as they froze.

"I'm not sure how these are used, or exactly what you put in them." Emmi reached over and flicked the top open. "But the cat, the one who Danced with you to find Susa, it came by and gave me some of its hairs and made it clear I was supposed to put them in the keeper."

"The cat?" Heron asked.

"Yes." Emmi dipped a finger in and brought out a few hairs—the cat's mingled with a longer one of her own.

"I'll never forget the cat anyway, but now I'll have more reason. That's the point of memory keepers." Heron brushed the hairs back in, finger soft as they stroked hers. "Not so much *what* one puts in, as it all gets mashed together in the end, as the fact that one *has* put something in. Sometimes it's just a comfort to hold, to think of the people who gave you things. Some people claim to relive memories when they touch the contents, but I never have."

"You put them in?" Emmi asked, drawing back. "Others don't put them in for you?"

"They can, but usually one puts things in themselves."

"The cat hair isn't the only thing I put in." Emmi shrugged.

Heron rose to their knees opposite her. Warmth poured off them as their eyes gleamed in the light. The mantle fell from their shoulders as they set the cup aside.

"There's a little of my hair, and Susa's too."

"*Your* hair."

Flickers of energy ran along Emmi's scalp and down her neck as Heron traced the line of her head, her hair.

"I know you have a memory keeper already," Emmi said, "but I thought maybe this could be for new memories with us."

"What are you offering?" Heron's hand slid down her shoulder as their other rose to clasp hers together. They still held the memory keeper, which pressed against the back of her hand.

"This is the start of courting, right?" Emmi asked, unsure what they meant. "It starts with a gift that symbolizes what we—I —want?"

Heron's grasp tightened. "What is it you want?"

"There isn't the same thing about rituals and formalities and clarity in Codaros." She shrugged. "We just sort of fall into things, or step in, and muddle around."

Heron loosened their hold just long enough to set the memory keeper on the ground between them, stars bright. "Yes, but you are offering a memory keeper, which means you have something in mind, or in hope. Even after all you now know of me."

"I like what I know of you." Emmi twisted her wrists, shifting so that her hands alternated with Heron's, each with one outside and one inside. "Your care for the home of your birth and the home of your choice."

"At least tell me what you want of me."

The plea for clarity hit Emmi hard, making her swallow the first answer that came to mind—themselves—and dig to offer them something to match all that they'd shared with her. "Honesty. " As they'd just given. "Comfort, a home."

"A partner?" Heron asked.

"In all ways, but I don't come alone."

"I will love Susa. I do already." Heron pressed her fingers, leaning in so their breath was warm against her cheek and lips.

"She has a birth father, and she likes you as a friend, hers and mine. Yet, tt won't be easy becoming a third parent." All the warning Emmi would give Heron. If they didn't know by now, or didn't care, no sense pushing.

"Do you want other children?"

"Maybe one or two, though if we don't, I've no quarrel." Emmi slumped, head tilting to one side the better to watch Heron's expressions. "But if I were to have more children I'm not sure I'd want to take them along with the court on progress."

"I won't be a princess forever, so I can leave court or become a musician or teacher in Tharis or Yaras, if that would suit." Heron smiled, a movement she felt as much as saw. "Though Amara said after your help with the Dance to find Susa the other night, perhaps you'd like to train to be a compeer and Dance with me for a few years."

The possibility struck Emmi as though from nowhere. Her, a compeer? Too strange a notion to consider much, especially when she and Heron had inched ever closer to the point that only the memory keeper separated their knees. Their bodies aligned, placing her head in the right position to turn sideways and up close to their lips.

Heron's head lowered slowly as they cupped her cheek again. "So many possibilities. Such a wonderful future together."

"Yes," Emmi breathed the word into Heron's mouth as she leaned in for a kiss.

❧ 25 ❧

Heron squeezed Emmi's hand, glad to see the spires of Tharis growing larger as the Marchon's progress neared the end.

Autumnal breeze whisked around the long, drawn-out stretch of walkers and wagons. Every footstep farther north brought them closer to the onset of winter. Equally, each step meant being that much closer to the end of endless movement and months of cuddling together against the chill. Ample reason to welcome the end in sight. They wore the warmest tunic and mantle they'd carried south in the spring, soft lengths of deep purple and pale gold well-suited to the weather. Thin wool socks protected their toes under sandal straps. Yet all paled in comparison to the warmth of their hand clasped in Emmi's.

Tharis made for a lovely image, too, with the castle spires stretching high into the sky—and yet dwarfed by the mountain peaks further north. Tall stone walls ringed the city proper, but it had long since overgrown and spilled along the riverfront and the roads leading to the great gates. Residents lined the road in ever-larger clumps, cheering the return.

Then again, they were always equally happy to cheer the departure of court in the spring.

The part of Heron that had served Kitiva as a messenger scanned the watching faces for signs that they welcomed the court's return as much for the money sure to pour forth as the castle filled with people needing food, new winter clothes, and more.

Heron-the-princess understood that they also welcomed the immediate presence of the princesses—the surest power to keep the city and fields safe against the blizzards that would inevitably cascade down as the temperatures dropped. One of the first Dances they'd ever described and sent back to Kitiva was on easing the blast of snow so that it did not choke narrow city streets.

Still, this return Heron viewed Tharis in a new light—as a possible future home. Not merely a base for a few months, but somewhere to stay. In a few years, when they retired from the princess ranks, they and Emmi might settle here, close to her family, especially if Emmi could lure her brother back north.

A tunic and mantle as fine as Heron's adorned Emmi, in shades of dark green and yellow contributed by Amara and Gisela. The other princesses and compeers thronged around, smiling and waving at the crowd. No one made any comment on Emmi and Susa in their midst. Indeed, Zora had been generous over the past weeks offering tips to Emmi as to how to partner Heron, as though Heron had never been dragged before the Marchon and accused of treason.

Thin, nimble fingers inserted themselves between Heron and Emmi's hands, pushing the two apart. Susa grabbed hold of each, wiggling as she marched with them to either side. Pride in her new long tunic shone from her, no matter that it had been passed down from her mother and much hemmed in the process. Heron glanced over at Emmi and shrugged. She smiled but cast a minatory glance down at the girl.

Susa had adjusted to the new situation a good half of the time. The rest she showed flickers of jealousy, though it wasn't always clear if she resented Heron's taking some of her mother's attention, or the time Heron devoted to her mother.

Yet in all, Heron felt so much more a Codaran than when they'd left Yaras.

After they entered the city walls and began to approach the palace, the progress's careful order started to break down. Members of court slipped off to join family or friends left behind, particularly those who didn't reside in the castle.

Susa tugged at Heron and Emmi's hands, yanking them off to the side.

"It's dada and aunt and uncle and the cousins!" Susa leaned forward, her whole weight bent toward a small knot of people in front of a gaily painted building.

Bright swathes of orange and green covered plastered spaces between the regular lines of blue shutters at each square window. The colors outlined an immense mug spilling over with bubbly drink and a platter dotted with pastries. Higher above was painted with a sleeping figure in a canopied bed. Sure sign of an inn and restaurant.

Against such a backdrop, the people made for a much humbler appearance. They wore long orange aprons over green tunics, even the two younglings smaller than Susa clinging to their parents' skirts.

"Go on." Emmi tapped Susa's hand and withdrew her fingers.

Heron pulled theirs away, too, rubbing the sore hand that Susa had clamped hard on. They paused as the girl raced over and vanished in the flurry of orange and green skirts and aprons.

Then stumbled to the side as Emmi yanked them out of the way of the progress. Amara, Gisela, and Stevan waved as they headed for the castle.

Wheels creaked as wagons piled high with trunks headed to the castle side yards, but there was a strict order of removing items. Heron's trunks, and Emmi's, would be delivered to their chambers without their lifting a finger.

All of which left Heron no reason not to follow Emmi over to the inn to meet Susa's father. They buried their chilly hands in folds of their mantle as the bowed and nodded, unsure of their reception or how Susa's father might view the change.

Only to shiver with pleasure as Emmi introduced Heron as her partner—and no one blinked an eye.

There might be bumps in the road ahead, but there would be easy spots as well. Heron slipped an arm around Emmi's shoulder, watching the last of the wagons roll on to the castle—and filled with surety that, like the wagons, he and Emmi would roll on to the end.

⚘

EMMI LEANED AGAINST HERON AND WATCHED AS HER FORMER LOVER and the man's family welcomed Susa back. Susa's father made a big deal over little things as always, but focused on Susa and how much she'd changed, and how well her clothes did and didn't fit her, and what she'd eaten, with little attention for Emmi or Heron.

So much easier to watch the drama knowing that it wouldn't swallow her whole. With every week that passed, Emmi was more and more comfortable in the quiet, easy sharing of her relationship with Heron.

Habit kept Emmi present as greeting Susa took so long that the progress vanished into the castle and the crowd started dispersing from the street.

Shadows grew and cool breezes rubbed against the parts of Emmi not pressed close against Heron.

And she realized she could leave. It was no longer a choice between being a shadow haunting Susa's father's family or going to her lonely, Susa-less room in the castle. Or, equally lonely, face the long trek out to the town up close to the mountains where the rest of her family lived. This year, she'd have company regardless.

Although, with her change in station to compeer, she wasn't sure where her room in the palace would be, or if she'd share with Heron.

"It's time we went on." Emmi bent and gave Susa a last hug.

"You're leaving?" Susa pouted.

"You can come to the palace to see me, just send word ahead so I'm there to greet you." Emmi stroked her daughter's hair. "But don't you want to be with your father?"

"Oh, darling daughter, will you leave me already?" Susa's father struck a dramatic pose, one hand across his eyes.

Susa hugged Emmi and then rushed to throw her arms around her father.

Emmi dabbed a tear or three from her eyes as she turned away and forged through the streets to the castle.

"I'll miss her too." Heron wrapped an arm around Emmi's shoulders, matching their steps to hers.

"You realize she'll be as dramatic as the rest of them when she's with us next?" Emmi sighed and nestled closer.

"If it's what she likes . . ." Heron shrugged.

Emmi leaned in and lowered her voice, even though growing distance made it unnecessary. "I'm so glad it's not what you like."

Heron glanced back and gave a mock shudder.

No sooner than they passed through the castle gate than they had to dodge piles of trunks and attendants dashing hither and yon to deliver them. Emmi's fingers twitched to dive into the chaos and extract her and Heron's belongings, but it wasn't her task. She followed in Heron's wake as they skirted along the exterior wall. "Do you know where I'll be rooming now?"

"With me? You know how large my chamber is." Heron smiled down at her as they led the way, though she knew it quite well. "There's ample space for us all, and we can add a truckle bed for Susa with ease."

"We won't need it that often." Emmi pressed their hand, a new, anticipatory warmth rippling through her veins.

"What?" Heron asked.

"Didn't you realize? Susa lives with her father's family when we're in Tharis," Emmi said. "She'll come to visit often, but usually for an afternoon and only rarely overnight."

Emmi had told Heron. They'd discussed the matter—but just as the change in her chambers to share with them hadn't really dawned until now, so too Heron hadn't fully absorbed the fact that they'd have the chambers to themselves without a wiggly young girl who'd developed an unwelcome ability to wake whenever Emmi and Heron snuck in extra kisses.

She wasn't surprised when Heron hurried them through the halls to their chamber.

Emmi paused a few steps in. Locked trunks lined one wall, a mix of those brought from the south and those left last spring. Those left were topped with cushions that needed plumping before they could serve as seats. The thick curtains at the windows had been beaten and were mostly free of dust, but there were spots where threads frayed. Similarly, the warm tapestries covering the outer walls showed signs of wear in places.

She blinked. Forced herself to view the space with a new eye: as something to share with Heron rather than space that she'd tend.

Whoever had prepared the chamber had taken the time to make the wide bed in the far corner and heap it high with blankets. Warmth radiated from the tidy blue-enameled stove against the far wall. A pitcher of spiced water rested above, filling the room with welcome.

Movement made Emmi blink and refocus on Heron. They stood near, arms extended and a thin, dark object resting on their open hands.

By now, Emmi knew the outline of a memory keeper on sight. Yet this was different. Heron's two keepers hung from cords around their neck, but this was thinner and longer. Spirals of gold wrapped around the dark gray cloth exterior, ending in thick caps that unscrewed from each end to access the single empty space at the center.

"It's lovely, but . . ." Emmi turned to study Heron's solemn face. "Do you need another?"

"It's meant for two to share." Heron held it out.

Emmi took it, jolting at the unexpected weight. The interior turned out to be made of gold, not just the spirals around the outside.

"To make memories together," Heron said, "and keep them together, with care, and hold them close so long as both live."

"You want us to share a memory keeper?"

"We are Codarans, where any may make an offer, not Kitivans where all flows from the woman." Heron sank to their knees. "I wish us to wed, when you're ready, and bind our memories and futures together."

"You haven't met my family, other than Aurel." Emmi clutched the new memory keeper close as she sat on a trunk and leaned into Heron.

"Nor you mine, other than Stork, but we are *of* our families, not *them*." Heron brushed a quick kiss across Emmi's lips. "We can make a new one here with ties to the old." They yanked a hair from their head and held it out.

Emmi matched the gesture, wincing at the quick sting.

They twined their hairs together and slipped them into the keeper, each closing their own end.

Then sealed their agreement with a kiss, or three, or five, or more, losing count in the shadows of night and the warm comfort of the bed.

❧ 26 ☙

No matter how surprised at how the world had turned, Stork had no defense against the joy flowering around him.

Flowering in truth despite the chill wind rattling the long bank of windows that formed one wall, and heralding winter's arrival despite the bright noonday sun. A sea of flowers bedecked the floor, their tiled blooms forming a mosaic from wall to wall. A matching mosaic of flowering vines covered the long interior wall. The vines crept up onto the edges of yet a third mosaic stretched across the ceiling with flowery stars peeping down through the pink and orange clouds of dawn. This was one of the Terparchon's favored reception chambers, and it showed.

Tucked in a corner, Stork wore his best attire, from thick socks lining well-polished boots to green breeches carefully brushed before donning, to a burgundy knee-length tunic. The symbol for Kitiva and citizens' duty to their home was emblazoned on the back of the tunic, while a gold medallion in the same form rested against the front. A matching gold-trimmed burgundy hat with a high peak kept his head warm and a gilt belt wrapped his waist.

Nevertheless, his finery paled in comparison to the crowd around. Stork was relieved that everyone seemed to have sensibly chosen shoes or boots, as he had on occasion witnessed northern Codarans pairing thick socks and sandals in snowy weather. Still, both courtiers and attendants wore layered tunics topped with warm mantles heavy with fringe or embroidery, as did Emmi's family come in from the countryside in bolder, less decorated styles but no less festive. Stork was the only one in sensible breeches.

Between the crowd and the stoves inserted in the fireplaces at either end, the room was quite comfortable. The flowers on the tiles covering the stoves didn't match the mosaics, but one could barely see them anyway given the platters of food resting atop them to keep warm. Savory scents filled the chamber, only half of which Stork recognized despite his many years traveling around the land.

Outside, the absence of clouds to the east suggested decent weather the next day. Just as well, since Stork planned to head across the river first thing the next morning, the better to reach Kitiva before serious winter snows made travel difficult.

Despite the onset of winter, he hadn't been able to resist attending the celebration of his nephew—nibling? Such a word!—and chosen beloved.

The music was not to Stork's taste, being a mix of drums, flutes, and harps, and all in harmony with each other. Pretty, yes, but Stork preferred crowds singing at the top of their lungs. No one was singing here, not so much as a word.

Still, joy fairly emanated from Heron—who'd beamed and hugged Stork earlier, right after their joining ceremony. Layered tunics in green and gold covered Heron's lean body, and more gold flashed from his— their—wrists and ankles. Two memory keepers swung from chains around their neck, the chimes lost under the melodic strums from the harp. They danced with Emmi, matching them in similar layers of gold and green. She smiled up at Heron, who glowed back, and every glance equaled a kiss.

Stork was careful to remember every bit of poetic description—no matter how florid—that came to him as he absorbed all details of appearance and clothes and dance. He'd have to describe everything to Heron's parents and the rest of the clan.

"Still trying to steal them back?"

Stork tensed, only half easing as he recognized Rik, the royal attendant and confidant, who'd snuck up on him. Though the sneaking wasn't too hard in this all-too harmonious and hence distracting ruckus.

In most respects Rik blended in with everyone else—average in height, build, skin, and of an indeterminate age. White hairs mixed with green and brown in their stubby braid; otherwise they could be Heron's age or Stork's. Their accent resembled the Marchon's most of the time, bringing a bit of mountain ululation amidst the general drawls.

And they were most definitely a *they*, an eleee as they'd made very clear the first time they welcomed Stork to the Codaran court, long before Heron's unexpected appointment as a princess.

They served the Terparchon and Marchon, and even spoke with their voice on occasion.

Stork nodded, and met Rik's gaze with his own determination. "Heron will return to Kitiva."

"To show Emmi around, and Susa, but they won't stay," Rik said. "They belong with us."

"If you're so sure, why push the point?" Stork might agree but refused to concede. He tapped his chest. "Heron belongs to us as much as to you, and always will."

"But they've found happiness and contentment here that escaped them before."

"That I can agree with." Stork shrugged. No matter how fun, this was not the time or place to engage in a lengthy debate. "I'm not here to steal them, but to absorb memories to take back and share a little of this joy."

He drank in the scene as other attendees flooded the dance floor in twos and threes to form patterns around the central couple.

Over in the opposite corner, Heron's new all-but-blood daughter beamed in pleasure, green tunic skirts the same shade as her mother and Heron, as she danced with . . . a cat? Yet the cat was quite graceful, in truth. The silver markings on face and tail shimmered as it curvetted around the girl. Heron had suggested Stork pass word to the

Kitivan princess to study the dances of cats and find in them ways to defend or attack.

Stork would tell her as much, and tried to watch the cat himself. Yet he found he couldn't keep his eyes on the beast, no matter how sweetly it played with the young girl, because Heron and Emmi drew his gaze again and again with their sheer joy.

Despite himself, Stork was glad for them. When he returned to Kitiva he'd report to council—and to his sister and the rest of the family.

Heron might never come back to Kitiva to stay, though they'd promised to visit, but they'd found a different kind of home with Emmi. A home of love and choice, of dance and laughter, of children and cats.

۞

IF YOU ENJOYED A SPY PRINCESS WHY NOT SIGN-UP FOR ALEA HENLE'S newsletter at https://BookHip.com/PCSWMCK and be the first to know when the next Dancing Princess book is released?

ABOUT THE AUTHOR

Alea Henle writes non-fiction by day and fiction by night. Contemporary and historical fantasy, fantasy romance—and more! Check out her website www.aleahenle.com.